MONSTER HUNTERS UNLIMITED

FLYING FIENDS AND GRUESOME CREATURES

BY JOHN GATEHOUSE AND DAVE WINDETT

Pe

PSS!
PRICE STERN SLOAN
An Imprint of Penguin Random House

For James Murphy (T.V.T.) & Bullet the Dog—JG

For all the readers and fans that I meet at comic conventions—DMW

And for Mandy Little of Watson, Little, Ltd. without whom,
this series would not exist—JG & DMW

PRICE STERN SLOAN
Penguin Young Readers Group
An Imprint of Penguin Random House LLC

Library of Congress Cataloging-in-Publication Data is available.

ISBN 978-0-8431-7028-3

10 9 8 7 6 5 4 3 2 1

INTRODUCTION

Monsters are real, and ghosts are real too. They live inside us, and sometimes, they win.

Stephen King—horror & fantasy author (b.1947)

Horror films are like cartoons for kindergarten kids compared to the nonstop tsunami of guts, bones, and brains that fill these blood-splattered pages!

So if you upchuck at the sight of a mere *pinprick* of blood, this book is definitely NOT for you!

Considering that we're dealing with some of the most savage, deranged, insane, maniacal supernatural teratoids (grotesquely deformed monsters) that have ever stalked this planet, prepare yourself to read detailed descriptions of flayed flesh, squished eyeballs, and disemboweled steaming human intestines! (*Psst!* DON'T show this book to adults—we don't want to be blamed for giving you psychotic heebie-jeebies-inducing nightmares!)

Reckon you've got what it takes to fight monsters? Ghosts? Vampires? Aliens? Demons from the dark dimensions? Then the International Federation of Monster Hunters needs YOU!

While the rest of whimpering humanity cowers indoors, squandering their pathetic little lives on moronic social-media networks and playing mindless computer games, you'll be knee-deep in guts 'n' gore as you battle against dangerous and deadly unnatural, undead hellions whose only aim is to feast on the festering fat of mankind!

And we'll be with you every step of the way!

This book is a top secret monster hunter's manual bursting with all the latest intel you'll need to survive an encounter with the hundreds of demonic denizens that dwell within the shadows of day and the stygian darkness of night!

Listed within the pages are over fifty—yes, fifty—of the most malformed mutations that exist worldwide! (One of the perks of monster hunting is that you get to visit some totally cool countries, catch a tan—or some frostbite—and experience other cultures and people!)

The kind-of-a-downside is that there's a good chance they'll be bringing you back home in a wooden box after you've been brutally torn to shreds by whichever satanic archfiends you've tracked down! But hey, what's life without a few chuckles, eh?

We'll supply you with detailed descriptions of what these bugly (butt-ugly) bogeymen and bogeywoman actually look like and what their powers are!

After all, if you attack the Chilean volcanic magma monstrosity Cherufe with a flamethrower, you're only going to make him stronger!

Also, we'll give you the best ways to defeat, capture, or destroy these fiends! Surprisingly, some of most terrifying terrors are total wimps! The Nordic aquatic abomination Nøkken might drown and eat you, but he can be easily killed by . . . a needle!

Then there are others—like the child-torturing (and eating) Tall Man—who are totally unkillable! (But at least you'll know you're going to die *before* you go into battle, which is always a help, right?)

Each chapter includes a case study featuring reports from celeb monster hunters like thirteen-year-old Tobias Toombes and our favorite fifteen-year-old Aussie girl, Soul-Gon McDonald!

Investigative reporter Neela Nightshade brings us another thrilling exclusive about her encounter with the sinister Jamaican Duppy, Victorian steampunk heroine Lady Theodora Bennett faces death at the hands of homicidal goblin Red Cap, teen Dhampir Karmilla Darkskye battles undead forces in India, and we reveal sixteenth-century monster-hunting monk Friar Jacob's continuing battles with the unholy!

There are fact files galore, encapsulating the most important info on all the Flying Fiends and Gruesome Creatures you're likely to run into!

And there's MORE! Monster hunters are very intelligent, so there's a couple of mad facts relating to each chapter that you can use to impress your buddies and teachers!

Did'ja know that the human ribcage expands and contracts *ten million times* a year? Wowsers!

Or that to reach to reach the center of the Earth you need to travel straight down for 3,963 miles? (Better pack those hiking boots!)

It's said that the Rotokas people of the Solomon Islands have the world's shortest alphabet with only *twelve* letters?

And that lead is a deadly, cancerous poison. Once released into the atmosphere it remains *forrrevvverrr*! Thanks to greedy car manufacturers and gas companies who in 1923 added lead to gasoline to save money, we now have *625* times more lead in our blood than people did pre-1923! (Gee, thanks, dudes! Much appreciated!)

Or that Sterculius is the Roman god of poo! (Straight up!)

We also give you some unusual words to help expand your vocabulary! (You wouldn't be reading this book if you didn't love words!) Such as . . .

Paraaskavedekatriaphobia—love that tag—is the fear of Friday the 13th!

Kakidrosis is stinky body odor!

Rhinotillexomania is compulsive nose-picking!

A macroverbumsciolist is someone who is ignorant of large words!

And loads more!

Make sure you send us YOUR blogs, tweets, instant messages, photos, artwork, blogs, film recordings, etc., about your blood-splattered clashes with the world's worst malefic mis-creations!

What are YOUR scariest monsters? Create a Monster Fear Factor Top Ten chart of the scariest—and the wimpiest!

So sharpen your battle-ax, recharge your neutron blaster, and go get 'em, tiger! The monsters are waiting for YOU!

DISCLAIMER: Anyone who goes monster-hunting does so at their own risk. We cannot be held responsible for our readers turning into vampires, werewolves, zombies or assorted nasties.

TABLE OF CONTENTS

FLYING FIENDS

To him who is in fear, everything rustles.

Sophocles—Ancient Greek playwright

(c. 497/6–406/5 BC)

So the big question . . . where do all these flying fiends you're about to track down and bloodily battle to the death come from, anyhow?

Well, the earliest airborne creature so far discovered is a 0.2-inch, six-legged, four-winged insect similar to a dragonfly known as *Rhyniognatha hirsti*, he of the disease-spreading bite!

This critter was looping-the-loop above the fetid steaming swamps of planet Earth between 320 and 400 million years ago, give or take a weekend off.

But the first genuine flying fiend is the ginormous dino-bird *Pelagornis sandersi* that lived around 25 to 28 million years ago,

This long-jawed, bony-toothed horror had a wingspan of between twenty to twenty-four *feet*!

Humans have been trying to take to the skies ever since a member of the *Orrorin tugenensis* crew (one of our earliest distant cousins—and possibly the first with an opposable thumb—who were chilling out in Africa millions of years ago!) saw a monster bird fly past overhead, grabbed two large palm leaves for wings, and leaped off the nearest cliff to give chase!

And we've been making equally crazy attempts to fly ever since!

In AD 1010, the totally nuts but kinda cool mad monk Elmer tied "wings" to his hands and feet and jumped from the top of the 431-foot Malmesbury Abbey in England—and flew for *six hundred feet* before smashing to the ground, breaking both legs! Ouch!

And if you think Wilbur (1867–1912) and Orville (1871–1948) Wright, aka the Wright Brothers, were the first people to fly—you'd be WRONG!

Back in 1853, English Lord, Sir George Cayley, sixth Baronet of Brompton (1773–1854) built a full-size glider, and ordered his poor servant to fly it!

Of course, every time we now take flight, we face a gruesome, bloody death at the hands of horrific supernatural flying terrors!

Like those gruesome Greek ghouls the Diraes, who turn their victims completely dribbling mad! Orang-Bati, the deadly Indonesian flying ape! And Yuki-Onna, the Japanese Snow Woman who freezes your very blood to solid ice!

Not forgetting murderous ghosts, cackling witches, crazy imps, devils, demons, and depraved vampires from your worst nightmares! And our all-time favorite, the omen of bloody death and destruction himself—the Mothman!

So hire a hang-glider, take to the skies, and good hunting!

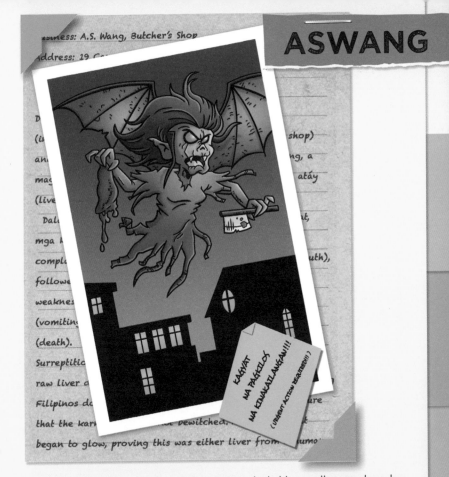

Business: A.S. Wang, Butcher's Shop
Address: 19 C...

(handwritten background text, partially obscured)

This section kicks off with the radically sick flying terror who holds a totally twisted number one supernatural horror celeb status in the Philippines, on par with that of the Western vampire and werewolf—Aswang!

These bloodsuckers are noxiously violent and fetidly foul, so make sure your bag of apotropaic gear (items used to fight evil boogers) includes salt, garlic, charcoal, coconut oil, and a bottle of calamansi juice, because you're gonna need them!

(Culinary note: Calamondin or Calmanansi—*Citrofortunella microcarpa*—is a citrus fruit tree that produces round lime-shaped fruit with an orange color when ripe. The skin is sweet while the juice is sour!)

Eyeball an Aswang in the daytime and they'll look completely human, often appearing as an old man or beautiful young woman with a dark complexion and lots of hair.

You'll usually find them running a butcher's shop, almost exclusively selling liver. But beware! That offal is either human flesh or Aswang, and if you eat it, *you* become Aswang!

Easy to recognize, Aswang have bloodred eyes, which comes from staying up all night hunting humans. Look deep into those eyes—is your reflection inverted (upside down)? Then that's definitely an Aswang!

They mainly operate on the thousands of islands in the Visayas region, which is one of three principal divisions of the Philippines.

(FYI: Portuguese explorer Fernão de Magalhães—aka Ferdinand Magellan [1480–1521]—landed on the Visayan island of Mactan on April 21, 1521. Learning of his insidious plan to bump off their well-loved king, Lapu-Lapu, the islanders were understandably majorly ticked off with ole Fernão, who got his just rewards when they speared and hacked him to death! Ha!)

When night falls, the Aswang transforms into a hideous ugly hag, although occasionally appearing as a cat, bat, bird, boar, pig, or dog to fool their intended victim. They kind of give the game away with their backward-facing feet and toenails reversed (the big toenail is on the small toe and the small one is on the big toe)! *Doh!*

Female Aswangs detach their torsos from the bottom half of their bodies and, sprouting wings, take to the skies in search of prey!

Topping their must-have shopping list of victims are young kids and pregnant women; these human-eating horrors are also partial to a rotting corpse or two! Delish!

Passing through the wall of a home belonging to an expectant mother, the Aswang flicks out its thin elongated tongue, piercing the sleeping woman's stomach.

With great delight, it sucks out both blood and growing fetus, before chowing down on the now (we seriously hope!) dead woman's liver and heart!

Monster hunter tip: Remember that coconut oil? If it starts boiling, an Aswang is close by!

Case Study 001/45A

Shock stat: Every year in the USA, there are around 78 million reports of food poisoning, with 325,000 people hospitalized and, give or take, five thousand deaths! (Wowsers!)

The U.S. Food and Drug Administration (FDA) agency was formed in 1906 to protect and promote public health. Among its many other tasks, it works hard to make sure that the food you eat is safe. Respect!

The Philippines have their own National Food Agency (NFA). Recently, there were reports of tourists dying from a serious outbreak of food poisoning on the Visayan island of Cebu in the Philippines. A federal agent was sent to investigate. Here is an extract of his shocking findings! (We've kept in a few words of Tagalog—the Filipino language—just because it's so cool!)

Business: A.S. Wang, Butcher's Shop
Address: 19 Cansayang Road, San Juan, Cebu
Date: Biyernes (Friday), 14 Disyembre (December)

Dalawang linggo (two weeks) into my pagsisiyasat (investigation) of the tindahan ng karne (butcher's shop) and I must conclude that the owner, a Miss A.S. Wang, a maganda (beautiful) young woman, is selling human atáy (liver).

Dalawang oras (two hours) after eating this foul meat, mga kaibigan (friends) of the afflicted say that they complained of tingling of the labi (lips) and bibig (mouth), followed by dizziness, problems with speaking and balance, weakness of the mga kalamnan (muscles), then pagsusuka (vomiting), diarrhea, and in extreme cases, kammatayan (death).

Surreptitiously, I sprinkled calamansi juice on the raw liver displayed in the shop, just as many country-living Filipinos do araw-araw (daily) before meals to make sure that the karne (meat) is not bewitched. As suspected, it began to glow, proving this was liver either from a human or the nakamamatay (deadly) supernatural creature, the Aswang.

Nagayong gabi (tonight) I watched as the owner, now changed to her true form of a pangit (ugly) old hag with mga pakpak (wings), flew out of the shop, returning with a fresh liver dripping fresh dugo (blood). I said a quiet panalangin (prayer) for the poor victim.

The authorities must close down this establishment and arrest the owner—agad! (Immediately!)

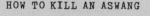

HOW TO KILL AN ASWANG

When the **Himalayan** peasant meets the he-bear in his pride,

He shouts to scare the monster, who will often turn aside.

But the she-bear thus accosted rends the peasant tooth
and nail.

For the female of the species is more deadly than the male.

"The Female of the Species" (1911)

This is the first of thirteen stanzas of a poem written by ace author and poet Joseph Rudyard Kipling (1865–1936), he of the classic *The Jungle Book* (pub. 1894).

The poem may sound like it's putting down women, but actually Rudy is writing in praise of their tenacity and courage! Righteous!

Far be it from us to suggest that women can, on occasion, be scary (think of your mom after you've trampled wet mud all through your home again!), but as our bodaciously bonkers series has often shown, some of the most hardcore and truly terrifying monsters out there are of the female variety!

And here's another demonically demented damsel to add to the list!

Banshees are found across Europe and North America, and if you eyeball one or hear her shrill screechings, it means that someone in your immediate family is going to DIE!

Paranormal investigators fight like bad-tempered Rottweilers over a bone as to whether the Banshee is one of the Undead, a Fallen Angel, a ghost, or an Unseelie fairy.

Why the confusion? Well . . . if you're out Banshee-spotting and happen to run into one, there's an odds-on chance you're next on her Death List, which means that any secrets of this melancholic apparition you might discover, get buried with you!

Their favorite country in which to scare the sweet bejeebers outta gentle folk is Ireland, where they're known as "Bean Sidhe" (from the Gaelic tongue) and "Bean Si" (from the Irish), both of which mean "woman/fairy of the fairy mounds," since it's a given that the batty broads originate from the "Otherworld," and "Bean Chaointe," a female keener—someone who wails before or after a death! Cheerful, aren't they?! Sheesh! Oh, and in case you are wondering, *bean* means woman!

These Banshees take the form of either a beautiful young woman with red eyes (from her nonstop boo-hooing!), a rich, middle-aged matronly type, or an ugly old hag, the three different sides of "Badhbh," Irish Goddess of Death and War! Mental!

Their preference in haute couture (high fashion) outfits includes a gray or white hoodie, or the grave sheet belonging to one of the unshriven dead (those who died without confessing their sins)!

In Scotland, they're known as "Bean Nighe" (the "washing woman") for their gnarly habit of sitting on the bank of a river washing the bloodstained clothes of those who are gonna soon be heading to the nearest graveyard!

To add to their Gruesome Factor, they've also been glimpsed washing severed heads and dismembered limbs moments before a terrible disaster strikes! Sweet!

Case Study 573/76B

Rudyard Kipling isn't the only homey to write fly lyrics in awe of womankind.
Wannabe teen hip-hop rapper DJ Ziiits came up with dis def ditty after what he
claims was a near-death encounter with da Banshee! (Pity his song bombed, but with
lyrics as vomitsville as this, we're not surprised!)

(Verse I)

Yo, yo, yo, word up, boyz 'n' galz in da 'hood

DJ Ziiits is here, righteous misunnerstood

I'm gonna school ya now, 'bout my new boo

She's supernova hot 'n' mos def coo-coo

A shorty who's ma angel, the soulless witch

A wack killa that makes ma heart twitch

(Chorus)

Banshee! When she appears ya end is nigh

Banshee! Hear her scream ya gonna die

Banshee! She's ma I-4-3, makes me wanna cry

Banshee-eee-eee!

(Verse 2)

When she busts a move ma gal's gonna make ya bounce
The Hereafter's waitin', ya death they will announce
She screeches, she wails, ya better start runnin'
Ya lifeline's gonna bail, fo sho tha's comin'
My Banshee's cray-cray, lady's cold as snow
She's totally off the chain, my 7-3-0

(Chorus, repeat twice)

For those not tight (cool) with rap/hip-hop slang, here's our phat (awesome) user-friendly guide!

"Word up"——Listen. "'Hood"——neighborhood. "School ya"——to teach someone something. "Boo"——boyfriend or girlfriend. "Supernova hot"——fantastic, the best. "Mos def"——most definitely, no argument. "Coo-coo"——mad, crazy. "Shorty"——girlfriend. "I-4-3"——I love you. "Bust a move"——to do something. "Bounce"——to leave quickly. "Bail"——to leave quickly, sudden death. "Fo sho"——for sure, for certain. "Cray-cray," "off the chain," "7-3-0"—— seriously crazy.

BANSHEE FACT FILE

Location: Ireland, Wales, Scotland, Germany, Scandinavian countries (Denmark, Norway, Sweden, Iceland, Finland, Greenland, Faroe Islands), North America

Appearance: Young, middle-aged, or old woman, various animal forms (see below)

Strength: Who needs muscle when you totally own the dreaded death-scream?!

Weaknesses: Cold-forged iron, salt. If caught, a Banshee has to grant you three wishes!

Powers: Shape-shifting (hooded crow, owl, raven, coyote, hare, weasel, stoat, etc.), flight, precognition (ability to see the future), Death Scream!

Fear Factor: If ya see or hear her, 100!!

WHAT TO DO WITH A CAPTURED BANSHEE

After a blood-soaked night of monster-killing, get her to wash the stains out of your clothes!

If you want to make a celeb rep for yourself in monster-hunting circles, one of the easiest (if most guaranteed-to-kill-ya!) ways to do so is to take up . . . vampire-slaying!

And one of the kookiest vamps inhabits the towns and villages of Chile in South America!

This aligerous (winged) nighttime terror doesn't just suck you dry of blood, it chows down on your saliva, phlegm, mucus, and snot, causing your body to dehydrate and die!

(Medical note: Disgusting though it is to accidentally blow a gooey green booger into your hand, this much-maligned gunk actually keeps our bodies protected. Mucus-producing membranes line the mouth, nose, sinuses, throat, lungs, and gastrointestinal tracts, stopping them from drying out. It also keeps dust and bacteria from getting into our bodies, and contains totally cool enzymes, protein, and antibodies to help fight off infection.

Our body produces between one to one-and-a-half liters of this stuff—every day!)

To the indigenous Mapuche people of south-central Chile, Colo-Colo is a soulless, shape-shifting cryptid that has the body of a serpent or lizard with rat features, short legs, oversize claws, and small, scale-covered wings.

Whereas to the south, the Chilote people, who live in the Chiloé Archipelago (on the *Isla de Chiloé*—the second largest island in Chile), think Colo-Colo looks more like a basilisk, with a serpent's body and rooster crest.

Elsewhere, to the Huilliche people, Colo-Colo has an elongated *mouse's* body with the *head* of a rooster!

When hunting this demon, check out darkened cracks or areas in a home, and listen for the wails of a li'l munchkin, because Colo-Colo makes a sound like a screeching human baby!

Also, sniff the air. Colo-Colo smells like rotting dead animal or fresh human excrement! Yum!

Its Thrill-Kill List includes hovering over its sleeping victims and biting the tips of their tongues, sucking out both blood and life force!

Or else sticking its elongated tongue up their noses and slurping on the snot and saliva, and feasting on the brains!

But Colo-Colo doesn't kill you quickly! It returns to feed from the same prey on a nightly basis for at least two weeks!

Its victims slowly become dehydrated and anemic (when a body suffers a reduction of red blood cells, causing tiredness and listlessness), until they fall into a zombie-like state, unable to think. They stand, unmoving, for days. And then—lights out!

The only way to rid yourself of Colo-Colo is to . . . burn down your house! (Kinda hardcore, but effective!)

Case Study 227/4CC

Eighteen-year-old Karmilla Darkskye is a
Dhampir (a child born of woman and vampire
and thus possessing vampiric powers) with
much dislike for her vampire father.

Karmilla keeps a diary detailing her deadly
battles with her father and his fetid Undead
army. Here is one such entry!

May 1—Chile.

Following my father's trail of bodies drained of blood—which I duly
dispatch with a swift beheading so as to check their rising again three days
hence—I arrive in Chile.

Here in a small farming village in Central Valley, south of the Bío-Bío
River, I find not my father but a group of villagers living in fear of one
of his pets.

Nailed to trees are "Wanted" posters written in Spanish, with a reward
offered for the capture or killing of Colo-Colo!

The village cacique (chief) informs me that eight village kids have recently
died after vicious attacks by this vampiric cryptid. I make a solemn promise
to rid the village of the creature's foul presence!

May 4

During my short stay with the Mapuche, I learn much of their ways. The
people grow maize, potatoes, beans, squash, and chili peppers, and keep
guinea pigs for meat.

Hunting and fishing are daily necessities. Llamas are kept as pack animals
and for wool. A villager's wealth is measured by the size of his llama herd!

Tonight my patience is rewarded. The wailing of a baby and the gag-
inducing stench of fresh feces emanating from an empty, darkened hut sends
my senses—acutely receptive to the presence of the feral Undead—into
overdrive!

The hideous creature, the size of a large cat but with rodent features,
flies out in search of prey!

"The only death tonight, vile vermin," I cry, swinging high my precious sword, Seraph, which once belonged to my hero, the mighty monster-hunter monk Brother Jacob, "is yours!"

With amazing speed, Colo-Colo dodges my attack! Screeching angrily, it lunges toward my throat, fangs ready to puncture my skin and turn me into a true vampire!

I turn swiftly, and upon seeing the symbol of the cross tattooed on my neck, it screams in twisted agony, its body bursting into flame!

Seraph cleaves through Colo-Colo's body, splitting it in two and sending its corrupt soul on a one-way trip—to Hell!

COLO-COLO FACT FILE

Location: Republic of Chile, South America
Appearance: Serpent-like with features of a rat and small, scale-covered wings.
Strength: Undead-ly!
Weaknesses: A spell cast by a Machi (a religious leader—usually an older woman—of the Mapuche); fire.
Power: Shape-shifting, flight, blood- and soul-sucking
Fear Factor: 88.6

EPICOOL USE OF COLO-COLO

Lure it into the air-conditioning vent of your school. The disgusting stink will waft into every classroom. Horrified health officials will close down the school for weeks while they try to locate the grody smell! Righteous!

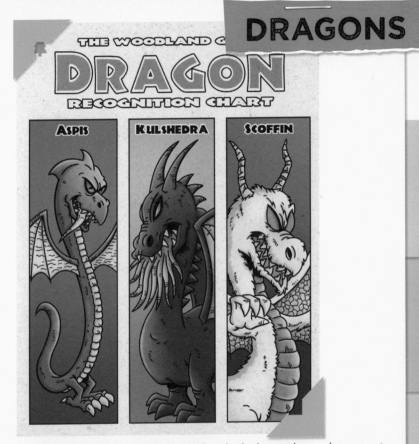

THE WOODLAND G...

DRAGON
RECOGNITION CHART

ASPIS   **KULSHEDRA**   **SCOFFIN**

Let's face it, everyone knows what dragons look like. They're big! With or without wings! Snakelike or reptilian! Kinda squamate (scaly)! Some breathe fire!

So we've chosen a few of our favorite phthartic (deadly and destructive), pestiferous (evil) flying reptiles/snakes to add to your monster-hunting list!

First up, the tiniest of all dragons! ("Whoa, dudes! You're kidding, right?" we hear you snort. "You've chosen the world's SMALLEST dragon?! Are you NUTZ?!")

Oh, ye of little faith! Some of the smallest monsters are the most dangerous!! Case in point—the terrifying Aspis!

Okay, let's quickly skate over his diminutive size, comparative to that of an overstuffed badger. What this li'l dude lacks in height, he sure makes up for in killer moves!

Sighted mostly around mountain and forest areas of the Iberian Peninsula, the Aspis has been variously described as having two feet and wings, being a quadruped (four legged) and winged, or having no wings (yet still possessing the ability to fly!).

They may be smaller than other dragons, but these tiny beasties sure pack one heck of a wallop!

Not only does a bite from Aspis-the-Dragon cause *instantaneous* death, its body is so filled with deadly poisons that even touching the skin of a dead one will have you pushing up the daisies!

Next up, catch a flight to Albania in southeastern Europe, where the terrified inhabitants shudder in constant fear of the demonic Kulshedra, the giant serpentine dragon that possesses four legs, two huge wings, horns, spines, and . . . um . . . *nine* tongues!

Aside from frying Albanians for dinner, Kulshedra also causes year-round droughts! And the only way to appease him is by . . . human sacrifice!

If tackling fire-breathing dragons isn't your thing, we suggest wrapping up warm and heading for the chilly North Atlantic Nordic island of Iceland. (Travel note: Size—39,768.5 square miles. Population—325,000. Average summer temperature—55.4°F/13°C. Capital city—Reykjavik.)

Here you'll not only find numerous mangy elves and trolls but also the petrifying, white-fur-covered horned dragon known as the Scoffin, whose eye blasts will literally . . . turn you to stone!

And finally, to round out your first dragon hunt, we've saved the pants-filling scariest until last!

Its handle might give you a clue! It's called . . . THE APOCALYPSE BEAST!!!!

This splenetic (ill-tempered) horror hasn't been sighted at Loch-Bel-Dracon (Lake of the Dragon's Mouth) for millennia, and we're kinda hoping it stays that way!

Because when it does eventually appear, supposedly on St. John's Day (on Midsummer's Day, June 24th, the day that celebrates the life of St. John the Baptist), it literally means: THE END . . . OF THE WORLD!!! *Aaaaiiieee!*

Case Study 1933/01D

Ranger Rich is the leader of the Junior Woodland

Rangers chapter of the Woodland Guild.

Aside from helping kids to gain their Woodland

Guild badges, Rich writes guides on various fauna and flora.

He has kindly allowed us to reprint the introduction to his latest publication,

"The Dragon Recognition Chart"!

Yes, my JWR buddies, dragons really do exist, and they're jolly easy to spot if you keep your eyes open and your heart pure!

While sightings in Europe and China are the most numerous, dragons have been seen worldwide for at least four thousand years!

Their image can be found on Aboriginal and Native American petroglyphs (carved rock drawings); on Babylonian landmarks such as Ishtar Gate at Al-Mahawil, Iraq (which shows the image of the snake-dragon, the patron god of Babylon); on Ancient Egyptian government seals and burial shrouds; on Mayan sculptures; on Peruvian burial stones and tapestries; and on Roman mosaics!

So anyone who scoffs at the existence of dragons is a fool, and as we know, JWRs are nobody's fool!

In China, dragons are called "Lung," of which there are four main types. The most famous is the T'ien Lung or Celestial Dragon, who guards the homes of the gods.

Then there's Shen-Lung, the Spiritual Dragon, who controls the weather; Ti-Lung, the Earth

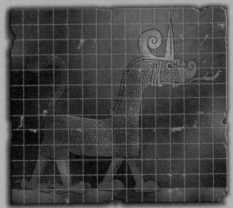

Dragon, who controls the planet's rivers and seas; and Fut'sang-Lung, the Underworld Dragon, who guards the world's most precious gems and metals!

   In this guide you'll meet lots of different dragons—but don't panic! I won't show you many evil ones, since I don't want to upset your sensitive nerves! We JWR members aren't called Nervous Nellies for nothing!

   Your Pal!

   Ranger Rich

DRAGON FACT FILE

Location: Lakes, rivers, seas, mountains, forests of the world!

Appearance: Two main types (although they tend to mix 'n' match): European dragons are usually reptilian with two or more legs, extra heads, small bat wings, and a serious bad attitude. Chinese dragons are often snakelike with two horns and no wings, and are intelligent and—mostly—sweet-natured. Whatever type, sizes range from four feet to the colossus below!

Strength: Well, the great Chien-Tang, commander of all Chinese river dragons, is nine hundred feet long, so we're guessing he's no pushover! And most of the others aren't ten-pound weaklings, neither!

Weaknesses: Counter-magic, or a sword made from cold iron (make sure that it's a verrryyy long sword, otherwise you're liable to get incinerated, crushed, or eaten!)

Powers: Fire- and/or ice-breathing, weather control, flight, magic, poisonous breath and skin. Good luck/bad luck power.

Fear Factor: 63.1

EPICFAIL USE OF A DRAGON

ER...IT WAS THE MARSHMALLOW YOU WERE SUPPOSED TO BE TOASTING!

Don't freak! You haven't been struck down by a sudden attack of rampant dyslexia—that really is the name of this Mephistophelian monstrosity!

(Medical note: Dyslexia—a developmental reading disorder—is a condition that causes reading, writing, and spelling difficulties, not just with words but also with numbers. Approximately 15 to 20 percent of the world's population has some form of dyslexia. Interestingly, self-made millionaires are four times more likely than others to have dyslexia!)

Word of warnin'! If you suffer from *ornithophobia* (a fear of birds) then you better go track down the Yeti instead, because this giant rapacious raven isn't for you!

The Gwagwakhwalanooksiwey—or "Gwag" for short—is a macrosomatic (gargantuan) -size bird that preys on the indigenous *Kwakwaka'wakw* people of Canada's Pacific

Northwest coast; most notably those on Vancouver Island in British Columbia.

His monstrous wings blotting out the sun, Gwak swoops down and plucks up a screaming victim before flying to his great house in the mountains, or to the North End of the World, whichever comes first. There he uses his long beak to peck out the victim's eyes before breaking open the skull and feasting on the brain! Yummy!

And Gwak's not the only abhorrent avian abomination the poor *Kwakwaka'wakw* people have to contend with!

Being the social sort, he invites his behemothic (gigantic!) bird buddy, Bakbakwakanooksiewae (his name translates to Cannibal at the North End of the World. You can figure out what *his* favorite pastime is!), and Bakbak's wife, Galokwudzuwis, to join the fresh-flesh-rendering party!

Galokwudzuwis (literally meaning Crooked Beak of Heaven) has feathers of black, white, and red, oval nostrils, and a spiral-shaped beak! Stylish!

The *Kwakwaka'wakw* people wear masks representing Bakbakwakanooksiewae and Galokwudzuwis in their annual winter Hamatsa ceremony, which is performed by both kids and adults in the hopes of appeasing these godlike predators.

Shame it doesn't work!

Case Study 991/45G

The first Prime Minister of Canada, John A. Macdonald (1815–1891), created the country's North West Mounted Police—better known as the Mounties—in 1873 to bring law and order to the wild North West Territories. In 1920, the organization had a name change to the Royal Canadian Mounted Police (RCMP).

Here's a report from a Mountie patrolling Vancouver Island who investigated a report of egg-stealing—and encountered an altogether different type of bird!

ROYAL CANADIAN MOUNTED POLICE——GENDARMERIE ROYAL DU CANADA

DIVISION	SUBDIVISION	DATE
"C"	Port Renfrew, BC	19 Dec 12

UNIDENTIFIED REPORT OF EGG-STEALING

Avatar Grove, Vancouver Island, BC

<u>DECEMBER 12</u>

I: At approximately 4:15 PM, this date, I was patrolling PR#6, crossing the bridge over San Juan River and continuing down Deering Road, when acting upon instructions from the Officer Commanding, Vancouver Island C/Div., I made my way to Avatar Grove, fifteen minutes from Port Renfrew. The OC had received a report that someone in Avatar Grove was attempting to steal eggs from the nest of the protected peregrine falcon.

2: Avatar Grove is a famous forested landmark of giant old red cedar and Douglas fir. Stepping into the forest is like stepping into some strange alien landscape, with tree burls (knotty growths) that are twisted and contorted into bizarre shapes. A burl on one red cedar measures twelve feet in diameter.

3: Making my way to Upper Avatar Grove I reached what locals dub "Canada's gnarliest tree," a giant red cedar with a trunk of forty feet. Close by was a juniper fir. It was here that I found evidence of an attempt to climb this tree.

Coils of rope, carabiners, snaps, and connectors lay on the ground.

4: Looking up, I spotted the suspect sitting in a tree harness, pulling himself up toward a large bird's nest some distance above. I shouted for him to come down.

5: I was waiting for the suspect to descend when a huge black shape appeared in the sky, blocking out all sunlight. A deafening sound assailed my ears, much like the hideous screech of a crow or raven and the flapping of bird wings amplified a thousandfold. There was much commotion above, followed by a distinctive human scream.

6: Another flapping of wings followed, and light returned. Staring up, I saw a giant black bird flying away. Something small was hanging from what looked like its talons. Of my suspect, all that remained was an empty harness.

Constable Ayasha LaKopp, RCMP

GWAGWAKHWALANOOKSIWEY FACT FILE

Location: Vancouver Island, British Columbia, Canada. (Travel note: Size of Vancouver Island—12,079 square miles. Capital city—Victoria. Population—765,000.)

Appearance: Giant raven with white eye sockets and red lips and nostrils.

Strength: über-über-scary!!

Weaknesses: Giant scarecrows! Gwak's terrified of them!

Powers: Super-speed flight. (Ornithology note: The Peregrine falcon is the world's fastest bird, reaching diving speeds of up to 242 miles per hour! The fastest bird at horizontal flight? The white-throated needletail—a large swift!—zips along at 105 miles per hour! Gwak slam dunks that record without even trying!)

Fear Factor: 81.1

TO DO WITH GWAGWAKHWALANOOKSIWEY

Kill it, stuff it, and donate it to the Edgar Allen Poe Museum!

(Literary note: Edgar Allen Poe [1809–1849] was an American author, poet, editor, and literary critic who created the detective-fiction genre. He wrote many awesome mystery and horror stories and is best remembered for the eighteen-verse gothic narrative poem "The Raven"! Totally rad!)

THE TRUE STORY OF THE **LINCOLN IMP**

Not all monsters are gnarly bloodthirsty freakazoids! Some are simply a pain in the butt!

Originating from Germanic Dark and Dingy Days of Yore (ancient times!), these invidious (unpleasant) critters are believed to be the demonic spawn o' Ole Horns 'n' Tail himself—da Devil! (Imps are the lowest-ranking of all demons in the infernal hierarchy of Hell!)

Other clever wits opine (hold the opinion) that they're twisted-to-da-max Unseelie fairies!

They're the hyped-up, wacked-out, cracked Hall o' Mirrors version of your bratty little bro or sis, and a kazillion times more annoying! (We know, hard to believe!)

Reaching the not-impressive height of one foot (give or take), these diminutive hellions look like deformed young kids with wings, and a pair of nifty horns growing outta their heads.

Imps (aka Emp, Hympe, Impa, and Ympe) are considered more mischievous than up-front evil, and some psychology "experts" even claim they're suffering from a revved-up peddle-to-the-metal version of ADHD.

(Medical note: ADHD—attention deficit hyperactivity disorder—is a psychiatric disorder that affects from 1–7 percent of kids, and three times more boys than girls. Symptoms include a lack of attention, hyperactivity, a low boredom-threshold, and impulsiveness. Or it could just be kids acting up, like kids do?)

WARNING!! Brats to the max, when Imps Go Wild, they'll smash up the home, poop in the fridge, swing from the chandeliers, and basically destroy your crib!

While imps do sometimes operate alone, they prefer to act out in a gang to make them look tougher than they really are. They dart from shadow to shadow, only glimpsed from the corner of the eye, leaving a painful prank to befall their victim!

Imps were all da rage way back when. Witches, magicians, and devil-worshippers commanded them with incantations to harm their enemies. In return for services rendered, witches allowed the not-so-cute-and-cuddlies to sup on their blood. Ah, sweet!

When witch trials were the go-to craze from the fourteenth to the eighteenth centuries, witch hunters would examine an accused witch to see if there were any marks on her body to indicate imp-suckling! If there were, then it was witch-burning time! Righteous!

The physician, botanist, alchemist, astrologist, and occultist Paracelsus (1493–1541), who was the dude who founded the discipline of toxicology (from the Ancient Greek word ΤΟΕΙΚΌΝ meaning "poisonous," it's the study of adverse effects of chemicals on living organisms), is reported to have kept an imp trapped in the crystal pommel of his sword! Like you do!

Case Study 505/031

One of the Devil's most famous imps can be found, of all places, sitting cross-legged atop a pillar in the Angel Choir inside Lincoln Cathedral in England. The dude's so popular, the town's soccer club is nicknamed the Imps, and his image appears on their club crest! Cool!

Local businessman and philanthropist James Ward Usher (1845–1921), a renowned jeweler and collector of expensive works of art, gave his fortune a major turbo boost when he gained sole rights to use the image of the Lincoln Imp in jewelry. People went mad cray for the merchandise! Even the then-Prince of Wales was seen sporting a Lincoln Imp pin! Respect!

To promote the town, the council recently created a flyer written by Impy himself, to teach kids the real story about the Lincoln Imp!

The True Story of the Lincoln Imp

Yo, Li'l Devils & Devilettes!

Impy the Lincoln Imp, here, to give you the lowdown on what REALLY happened in Lincoln Cathedral back in the fourteenth century!

If you believe those so-called "factual" websites, the reason I'm turned to stone atop a pillar in the Angel Choir is because I was up to no good!

Nah! Not me! I'm a total sweetie!

Some humes claim that me 'n' another imp, we was sent by our daddy (who you call SATAN! Really nice guy, once ya get to know him! I'll introduce you, if you like!) to cause havoc in some grungy town in the East Midlands called Lincoln.

Well, yeah, we DID go there, 'n' a few little incidents DID happen, but it wasn't MY fault! HONEST!!

So, long story short, we arrived at this totally freaky Christian religious house, which the humes first started building back in 1088 and finished four years later! For 238 years, from 1311 until 1549, it was claimed to be the biggest building IN THE WORLD!! Brother, did they think small back then! Sheesh!

We dropped in simply to say our prayers, because imps are BIG on prayers, when some silly lord bishop dude stepped on my foot 'n' didn't say "sorry."

Well, what would you do?

Understandably, I kinda lost it! First, I tripped up the old booger, then I pushed over the dean 'n' started annoying the verger (church official) 'n' the choir!

When I began smashing windows, this interfering angel appeared 'n' zapped me with dark magic, turning this cutie into stone!

And I've been stuck here ever since!

Your impish friend,

Impy

IMPS FACT FILE

Location: The world
Appearance: Holy terror punk with horns and wings
Strength: Puny!
Weaknesses: Magic spells, crystal, cold iron
Powers: Flight, immortality, power to grant wishes, teleportation
Fear Factor: 6.16

HOW TO SCARE OFF AN IMP

Lure it into a carnival House o' Mirrors and let it smash up the place, thereby giving it a kazillion years of bad luck!

There are 160,000 species of moth worldwide. But only one delish, evil *killer* moth—Mothman!

Some US government authorities suspect that Mothman is an unworldly creature of unknown origins . . . i.e., an *ALIEN FROM OUTER SPACE*!!

Or he may be a prophetic (sees into the future) being of death-dealing doom!

Whatever, Mothman made his debut appearance on the evening of November 12, 1966.

Five gravediggers, busy preparing a recent stiff's burial plot at a cemetery in Clendenin, West Virginia, glimpsed a "man-size creature" with huge wings fly out from some trees and over their heads!

Three nights later and forty-nine miles away, a group of four teens were speeding in their car to a nature reserve outside of Point Pleasant, West Virginia, to "party on down, dude!"

Driving past a former World War II munitions plant, they saw ahead a horrifying seven-foot-tall dark figure with glowing red eyes and wings!

Terrified, the driver slammed on the brakes, did an ultra-cool reverse 180, and got the heck outta there at a hundred miles an hour!

But to the friend's growing panic, the creature simply extended its wings, flew up into the air—and kept easy pace with their vehicle! It flew off only when the fear-sweat–dripping teens reached the safety of town!

Since then, there have been hundreds of Mothman sightings worldwide!

So . . . why the "alien" connection? Because at the time of the original sightings, there had already been a sharp increase in UFO (Unidentified Flying Objects) activity in the area of West Virginia!

(Space note: Scientists guesstimate—a guesstimate is a slightly flakier version of an estimate—that there are roughly 200 billion stars in the Milky Way galaxy alone, and approximately 60 billion *inhabitable* planets.

Of these exoplanets (planets outside of our own solar system), the closest so far discovered is *Epsilon Eridani b*, which is 10.5 light years away! A light year is the distance light travels in one year, which is roughly 5,878,625,000,000 miles—basically, six *trillion* miles!!—give or take a rest stop. Kind of far, then!)

As for being a Prophet o' Doom, Mothman was spotted on December 15, 1967, moments before the Silver Bridge over the Ohio River connecting the towns of Point Pleasant, West Virginia, and Gallipolis, Ohio, collapsed, killing forty-six people!

He was seen on April 26, 1986, at Chernobyl in the Ukraine, scene of the world's worst nuclear power-plant disaster, when dozens of workers were killed, and cancer deaths in the area increased dramatically!

And again in April 2002, in Tbilisi, Georgia, ahead of a deadly earthquake! Chilling!

"SO THERE'S A MOTH IN YOUR CLOSET, TIMMY? BIG DEAL!"

Tobias Toombes is a thirteen-year-old monster hunter who posts a weekly blog.

A MONSTER HUNTER'S BLOG

There I was, jostling with the masses at the annual Mothman Festival in Point Pleasant, West Virginia, hoping for an appearance by ole Lepidoptera Dude himself!

Suddenly, a hand lands heavy on my shoulder, squeezing hard. A gravelly voice rings out: "You're under arrest, creep!"

Time warp back an hour, homeys, and I'm arriving in town late afternoon with my folks to check out said festival, which takes place every third weekend in September.

Heck, there's even a Mothman Museum and a mondo-cool twelve-foot-tall stainless steel statue of the creature standing proud in the town center! Awesome!

Ya gotta admire the locals. Some suspected alien creepoid scares the sweet bejeebers outta 'em, and whadda they do? See a way to make a fast buck! Righteous!

While my folks went mental with a lame photo-fest, I slipped away, scanning the darkening skies.

That's when this weirdo dude makes a grab for me! Pulling free, I find myself face-to-face with a solid mass of muscle dressed all in black and fronting designer shades!

"Name's Hardy! Rock Hardy! CBI Special Agent!" he growled through gritted teeth. "That's the Central Bureau of Investigations to you, punk!"

"How do, homey?" I said, wiping the spittle that came with his halitosis-stinking words off my cheek. "Wassup?"

"This agent's been keeping watch on your blog!" Hardy hissed. "Trying to scare impressionable Americans with crazy stories of fake monsters is a federal offense!"

And that's when everything kicked off! People screamed in terror! There was a high-pitched angry screech above us! A massive shape swooped down, huge wings extended!

My heart skipped to see the hideous

sight heading straight for us—
Mothman!

The creature's piercing red eyes burned into my brain! My legs buckled! Mothman grabbed the Rock's arm, lifting him into the air!

Instinctively, I leaped, wrapping my arms around the government man's legs, pulling him free of Mothman's grasp!

We crashed to the ground! With a frustrated shriek, Mothman flew off into the sable night!

"This agent is grateful for your assistance, kid!" snorts Hardy awkwardly. "That giant eagle could have seriously injured this agent! All charges against you are summarily dropped!"

And with that, he faded back into the crowd!

Giant eagle?! Get real!

MOTHMAN FACT FILE

Location: USA, Mexico, Chile, India, China, Ukraine, countries in the Middle East—basically, anywhere that tragedy is about to strike!
Appearance: Seven-foot man-moth hybrid with freaky glowing red eyes!
Strength: Alien!
Weaknesses: Bright lights, giant can of fly spray!
Powers: Doom merchant!
Fear Factor: 96

HOW TO KILL MOTHMAN

Hire a helicopter, and as night falls and Mothman prowls the skies, release a giant mothball, crushing him flat!

MURDEROUS GHOSTS

THE ILLUSTRATED
Police *Gazette*

No. 1,876.   10th APRIL, 1899   Price One Penny.

THE GHOSTLY KILLER APPEARS

THE BLOODY KNIFE

CONSTABLE G.F. WILLM

Depending upon your beliefs, a ghost is either a person's "soul," "aura," "personality," or "life energy" that has somehow survived bodily death and is now trapped between this world and the Hereafter (aka da Spirit World!).

News flash: Not all ghosts fly (although most do); neither are they all human.

Inanimate ghosts include ships, trains, planes, tanks, and cars!

There are a kazillion ghost animals, and *all* types of human-y ghosts:

The "haunters" who float across a room wailing "Wooo-ooo-oooh!" and frightening no one other than an extremely timid hamster!

Ectoplasms—mist and fog blobs! Shadow ghosts who have no features, merely dark shadow shapes!

Apparitions! Doppelgängers! Lemures! Kobolds! Crowd demons! Dark entities!

And those gnarly cray-cray poltergeists—pesky, invisible delinquent spirits who invade homes and smash up the place!

But this chapter deals with one specific type of spirit—the mentally awesome, psychotic death-dealing ghosts!

These sanguinary (bloodthirsty) spooks generally met an unexpected and grisly death and have now returned from the yawnfest Nether dimension to enact horrifying vengeance upon the living!

Appearing in cultures the world over, these phonomaniacal (having a pathological need to kill) phantasms have many nifty ways of murdering their prey!

F'rinstance, in Venezuela, South America, *La Sayona*, the ghost of a beautiful young woman who haunts the city's highways, lures errant (misbehaving) husbands into her unbreakable grasp. Her head then transforms into that of a cackling, rotting skull, literally frightening the poor schnook to death!

The *Phi Tai Hong* of Thailand is a noxious specter of a person who was removed from the human gene pool in a blood-splatted death. It materializes where it died, killing any luckless passerby in the hopes that *his* or *her* spirit will take the spook's place in the Afterworld!

There's the Chinese *Shui gui*—angry water spirits of the accidentally drowned. They take bodily possession of a person and make them drown themselves!

While the poor Native American Navajo tribe have the grade-A insane *Chindi* to contend with, the ghost form of everything that was bad in a person!

These totally evil beings spread the dread "ghost sickness," infecting people with a death-dealing illness of which there is no cure!

GLOSSARY

We don't have room here to fill you in on *all* the terms used in ghost-hunting, but here's a few to get you going:

Eidolism: A belief in ghosts.

Electronic Voice Phenomena (EVP): Ghostly voices or noises caught on a recording machine!

Harbinger: A ghost *from the future* popping back to the present to warn of impending doom!

Hemography: That pants-filling moment when bloody stains, handprints, or footprints appear on objects—from nowhere!

Phantosmia: Some ghosts stink, and some ghost-hunters can smell them! Favorite ghostly *eau de colognes* include sandalwood, rose, and stinking rotten eggs!

Vortex: A specific focused center of ghostly activity, with blood-freezing cold spots and crazy electromagnetic disturbances!

Case Study 011/3MG

The *Illustrated Police News* (pub. 1864-1938) was a massively popular British tabloid newspaper.

It depicted in deliciously gory detail the most blood-soaked and depraved murders and macabre events of the times, including serial killer Jack the Ripper's reign of terror in the East End of London in 1888!

In 1886, the paper had the dubious honor of being voted "the worst newspaper in England"—and its circulation promptly skyrocketed!

Here's a report from a rival UK tabloid, the *Illustrated Police Gazette*, about an attack by a murderous ghost!

Killer Ghost Stalks The Streets
Bloody Atrocities in Somerset

IO April I889

An event of frightful proportions occurred on late Friday night last in the market town of Bridgwater, Somerset.

The particulars of this remarkable and singular shocking happenstance began at the half hour of eleven.

Police-Constable G.F. Willmetts was patrolling his beat along the thoroughfare of Lamprey Road, Bridgwater, when his attention was attracted to shrieks of bloodcurdling terror.

With the aid of his bulls-eye lantern, the constable at once perceived that the spine-chilling hullabaloo was emanating from the abode of Number 74.

Of a sudden, and according to the constable, "a tall, white female figure, with a countenance twisted in a most hideous rage, appeared to float through the closed front door, shrieking and gibbering as would an escaped patient from a lunatic asylum."

The figure, which Constable Willmetts immediately deduced to be a spiritual apparition, held within her grasp a bloody butcher's knife. With a final cackling shriek, the ghost passed through the shocked constable, who almost fainted from fright. Said ghost then dissipated into the nothingness of the Beyond.

Investigating further, Constable Willmetts found within said abode the body of a man in his late fifties, lying on the hall floor in a pool of blood

At present, the police have no suspects in this terrible murder.

MURDEROUS GHOSTS FACT FILE

Location: The world
Appearance: Take your pick!
Strength: Ghostly!
Weaknesses: Zap them with an exorcism! (An exorcism is a religious ritual that banishes ghosts and demons back to the Netherworld!)
Powers: Flight, intangibility, invisibility, wind power, body possession, telekinesis, and the ever-phenom—Death Scare!
Fear Factor: The murderous ones—79.6. The wailers? Pft!

HOW TO GET RID OF A GHOST

I SAID *EXORCISE THE GHOST* NOT EXERCISE IT!!!

What do you get if you cross a *hominid* (great ape) with a *chiropteran* (bat)? An Orang-Bati, obviously!

Found exclusively on Seram, the second largest of the Maluku Islands (aka the Moluccas) in Indonesia, the *über*-hideous child-devouring Orang-Bati has been eyeballed as standing four to five feet tall with a thickset furry primate's body, bloodred skin, large leathery wings, and a long thin tail.

These freaky-weirdos of nature live in caves inside Mount Kairatu, an extinct volcano situated in the dense and caliginous (dark and misty) mountainous rainforest.

At nightfall, and with heart-chilling mournful howls, they swoop down upon nearby villages, snatching up screaming children before flying off to enjoy a midnight feast!

Their name originates from the Indonesian words *orang* ("person") and *bati*, which has numerous meanings, everything from "brave warrior" to "gain" to "nightmare," but in this case doubles up as "man with wings."

(Nature note: Native to Indonesia and Malaysia, orangutans, with their distinctive shaggy reddish hair, are the most intelligent of the great apes. *Hutan* is the Indonesian word for "forest," so orangutan literally means "man of the forest." Sadly, evil profiteering humans, hell-bent on ecocide (the utter destruction of the environment), are tearing down the orangutans' precious rainforest homes in Sumatra and Borneo at a truly shocking pace, so these gentle giants are now listed as one of the most critically endangered species on earth, and by 2023 they could well be extinct. Yup, 2023! Sensing your lack of okay with that? Ours, too!)

The Orang-Bati first came to Western attention in the fifteenth century, when Portuguese missionaries popped over to the island to convert the locals to Christianity (whether they wanted to or not!).

God's warriors reported sightings of nocturnal "winged monkeys" (even though there are no monkeys on Seram!) or "giant bats" that filled the air with shrill screechings!

(Nature note 2: Funnily enough, there *is* a species of mega-bat on Seram! The Ceram fruit bat [aka Seram flying fox—*Pterpus ocularis*] is endemic [commonly found] to the Indonesian islands of Seram and Buru. Weighing up to 3.5 pounds, its wingspan can reach a colossal five feet or more! Yowsers!)

Case Study 565/20B

Bloodthirsty pirates have been hacking their way across the world's oceans for thousands of years.

The first documented pirate attack is found on an Egyptian clay tablet dating back to 1350 BC!

And killer Long John Silvers still kick butt today. The water around Indonesia is considered the most dangerous in the world for piracy!

We recently attended a séance by famed Romani psychic and spiritualist Aysi Kleerlee. She made contact with that totally infamous pirate Edward Teach (aka Thatch)—ole Blackbeard himself (1680–1718), who told of a terrifying encounter with Orang-Bati!

Transcript from a Madame Aysi Kleerlee direct voice communication

A SÉANCE WITH BLACKBEARD

Date: II October

Sitters: John Gatehouse, Dave Windett

Communicators: Edward Teach

KLEERLEE: Helll-lllooo! Can you hear me? (pause) Is there anybody there? (pause) Spirit, speak to meee. . . .

(Silence, then voice fades in)

BLACKBEARD: (gasps) Arrgh! Shiver me timbers! Who be addressin' Blackbeard, Scourge o' the Seven Seas! (growls) I'll slice ye in half, ye scurvy dog!

KLEERLEE: Calm yourself, Edward. I speak to you across the psychic waves. . . .

BLACKBEARD: (chuckles) Waves? Arrr, Jim lad! Ye be on a boat close by, then!

KLEERLEE: Um, quite. I've come to hear more of your battle with Orang-Bati. What took you to the island of Seram?

BLACKBEARD: (*snorts*) Well, wench, I felt th' hangman's noose o' th' Royal Navy tightening 'round me neck in th' Caribbean! An' since I had no wish to dance the hempen jig (*laughter*) I gives 'em th' slip an' sets sail on me ship th' *Queen Anne's Revenge* for Indonesia! I had booty to bury! Arrr!

KLEERLEE: That sounds exciting!

BLACKBEARD: One moonlit night we landed an' carried th' chest up th' mountains! (*groans*) I swear, lass, Hell's sewers are less inhospitable! (*hacking and spitting sound*)

Me crew had but finished th' task when this terrible screeching noise assaulted our ears. From out of th' darkness a huge flying ape appears in th' sky, all red o' teeth 'n' claw 'twere!

(*shouts*) "Prepare to repel boarders!" commands I, an' me men let off an almighty volley o' buckshot——(*growls*) but 'twere of no use! The Devil's pet swooped down an' ripped one man's face clean off with its deadly claws! Another man fell, his neck snapped from the demon's beating wings, whilst a third were speared by its deadly tail!

KLEERLEE: (*gasps*) Oh! How terrible!

BLACKBEARD: (*roars*) "Sink me! Back to th' ship!" I ordered, an' we ran back down th' mountain, the death cries o' me men ringin' in me ears . . . ! (*sobs*)

(*rages*) But if ye tell anyone o' this, ye picaroon, I'll keelhaul ye! (*screams*) Walk th' plank, ye will! Oooh arr! Arr, I say! Arr . . . ! (*voice trailing off*)

RECORDING ENDS

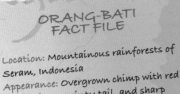

ORANG-BATI FACT FILE

Location: Mountainous rainforests of Seram, Indonesia

Appearance: Overgrown chimp with red skin, wings, pointy tail, and sharp teeth!

Strength: Prodigious!

Weaknesses: If one attacks, make a loud noise! It's kind of wimpy and will fly off!

Powers: Flight, scaring the bejeebers outta li'l kids!

Fear Factor: For small fry, 100!

WHAT TO DO WITH A CAPTURED ORANG-BATI

Hire it out to a movie production company filming a remake of *The Wizard of Oz*! (If you don't understand that reference, then go watch the original!)

Endangered Animals Fund Newsletter

July 29

ELEPHANT RESCUE!

Full Story - See Inside

The Gwagwakhwalanooksiwey isn't the only ginormaniacal (maniacally ginormous) mutant fowl that we spunky and kind of heroic (well, we are!) monster hunters have to take down!

For instance, there's the Greek man-eating Stymphalian birds, those avaricious avians of bronzed beak, razor-sharp metallic feathers, and poisonous poo!

The Hindu- and Buddhist-eating Garuda, with a wingspan *miles* long!

Or perhaps you fancy going mano a mano with the hellacious hardcore Native American Thunderbird, which can shoot out deadly lightning bolts from its eyes!

(Meteorological note: Lightning bolts strike the earth on average up to one hundred times *per second* and carry one BILLION volts of electricity! The bolts charge the air around them to 54,000 degrees Fahrenheit, which is five times HOTTER than the surface of the Sun!)

And then there's that Middle Eastern and African nightmare—the Roc!

How big are we talking about? Well, noted celeb world traveler Marco Polo (1254–1324) reckoned that "it was for all the world like an eagle, but one indeed of enormous size; so big in fact that its quills were twelve paces long and thick in proportion." How does a forty-eight foot wingspan grab you? Each feather twenty-four feet long and the shape of a palm leaf? Legs as thick as tree trunks?

An egg laid by a female Roc is an eye-watering 150 feet in circumference! (We do not want to even *go* there! Oww!)

Polo went on to relate that "it is so strong that it will seize an elephant in its talons and carry him high into the air and drop him so that he is smashed to pieces; having so killed him, the bird swoops down on him and eats him at leisure."

(Nature note: An elephant squirts out three hundred pounds of dung—the weight of an adult male gorilla—every day! If grabbed by a Roc, we can only assume that, in its terror, the creature will flush out the whole lot in one go! So if you're hunting Rocs and this happens, we advise not to be standing directly below! *Ewww!!*)

Case Study 909/48R

China imports 70 percent of the world's illegal ivory, which is used to make carved ivory objects and traditional Chinese medicines.

An estimated 100,000 African elephants were brutally slaughtered for their ivory tusks in just three years (2010 through 2012), the poachers attacking with military-style weapons such as hand grenades and high-powered machine guns.

One elephant is killed every fifteen minutes. At the current rate, in less than ten years there will be no more elephants left in the wild!

Thankfully, a number of conservation groups are trying to turn the tide on this horrific speciocide (destruction of an entire species).

Here's a field report from an activist working for the Endangered Animals Fund charity, on patrol with game wardens in the Serengeti National Park in Tanzania, East Africa!

The plaintive cry of a frightened elephant echoes across the lush rolling grasslands of Northern Serengeti. We are close to the 245-mile Mara River, the rest stop for migrating animals, as it snakes its way to Lake Victoria.

Chief Warden Belamri signals the driver to stop our jeep, indicating something ahead. Through binoculars, I spot an adult male elephant moving at speed across the bush. When threatened, an elephant can move up to twenty-five miles an hour!

Hovering above is a small helicopter, its occupants firing down on the terrified animal with deadly machine guns.

"Poachers!" growls Belamri as we race toward the elephant, knowing that our efforts will be in vain. The helicopter is diving in for the kill shot!

The sky darkens, the wind whipping up. And suddenly, there is a shriek so loud it threatens to burst my eardrums!

Shooting past us overhead at unbelievable speed is some type of enormous bird, larger even than a jumbo jet!

The furiously flapping wings create hurricane-force winds that strike the helicopter, sending it twisting in the air.

Lifting up my camera, I take numerous shots of this amazing beast.

"Roc!" gasps Belamri in admiration, watching the Roc grasp hold of the aircraft, crushing both it and its occupants in giant talons!

With relief, I watch the elephant make it safely to a thick forest of trees. The Roc, frustrated, flies off into the far distance.

"The Roc was not saving the elephant," explained Belamri later. "It simply did not want another predator after its prey!"

ROC FACT FILE

Location: Middle East countries; Madagascar, Southeast Africa. (Travel note: Half the birds and most plants on Madagascar are exclusive to the island!)
Appearance: Giant horror-bird of gargantuan proportions!
Strength: Go on, take a guess!
Weaknesses: Don't! Have! A! Clue!
Powers: Super-speed flight, super-powerful wing flapping!
Fear Factor: 71.9 (Or 100 if you happen to be an elephant!)

HOW TO EARN FROM A ROC

Stuff its molted (shed) feathers into giant pillowcases to sell to ogres to help with their beauty sleep! Because, for sure, they need it!

WILL-O'-THE-WISP

Hyenek Classification
DE-1 - Nocturnal Light

Date of Sighting ....Location ....
Notes

Cassandra's Guide to U.?

Next up on our hit list of monsters to zap are murderous critters that may be ghosts, fairies, witches, dragons, or, like Mothman, possibly unearthly in origin!

Some parapsychologists (scientists who investigate supernatural phenomena) claim that Will-o'-the-Wisps are the spirits of children who died unexpectedly.

Others argue that they are sorcerers or witches transformed into energy balls.

Or perhaps "fairy lights" carried by mischievous fairies to lead humans to their deaths!

While a growing number of investigators reckon they're UFOs (Unidentified Flying Objects) from another world, or even . . . another dimension! No kidding!

(Science note: In recent years, many a reputable scientist has calculated that our universe is but one of many, and that a multitude of universes in *alternate* dimensions—aka the

51

Multiverse—exist beside one another! Our universe, which exploded into being 13.5 billion years ago, and the observable part of which stretches for at least 46 billion *light years* in every direction, came perhaps from the collapse of a previous universe in a parallel dimension! We know! Mind-freakin' AWESOME!)

Will-o'-the-Wisps are global and go by a variety of handles: Jack-o'-Lanterns (USA), Boi-tatá ("fiery serpent"—Brazil), Min Mins (Australia), Brujas ("witches"—Mexico), Luz Mala ("evil light"—Argentina), Aleya ("marsh ghost-light"—India and Bangladesh), and Hitodama ("human soul"—Japan).

And the Brits call them Peg-a-lantern, Spunkies, and Hinky Punk, among many other cool tags!

They're usually spotted at night hangin' out in desolate, spooky, mist-covered wetlands, forests, graveyards, and ancient ruins such as deserted castles. These ethereal (unworldly) globes of light or fire are usually red, blue, yellow, green, or orange, their colors constantly fluctuating to either suit their moods or as a way to communicate with one another.

Unlike true light, Will-o'-the-Wisps appear to have substance. They avoid obstacles rather than passing through them (which kind of blows the theory that they're ghosts, wouldn't you think?!), or else they teleport from one side of an object to the other.

Whatever! The malevolent little creatures just want to kill you!

Waiting for someone to approach, they begin slowly spinning and weaving around in the air.

An unwary traveler, mesmerized by this luminescent light show, will irresistibly try to follow as they fly off, only to fall into treacherously deep marshes or mud bogs and be helplessly sucked down to a gruesome death!

Mirroring Mothman, Will-o'-the-Wisps gleefully appear in places where tragedy is about to strike!

And those seen in graveyards go by the tag "corpse lights," because it's said that they light the way to an approaching funeral—usually your own!

Case Study 855/7WW

Major shocker! Humans have been eyeballing UFOs for tens of thousands of years!

The first recorded sighting of a UFO appears way back in the time of the Egyptian Pharaoh Thutmose III (who reigned ca. 1479–1426 BC).

Papyrus documents reveal that countless large "circles of fire" kept appearing for many days above the pyramids, and that they "shone more in the sky than the brightness of the sun".

There were numerous UFO sightings in Rome in 218 BC, once every twelve years in fourth century China, and hundreds times more in Germany and Switzerland in the sixteenth century!

These days, thousands of UFOs are sighted yearly worldwide, the majority eyeballed hovering over North America.

Dozens of reputable (and some decidedly dodgy!) UFO groups keep track of them all, many with the help of UFO spotter guides!

Here's a recent diary entry from one such American UFO-spotter!

July 4, 11:47 PM,
the Everglades, Florida

The 'Glades were first inhabited 15,000 years ago. But tonight, it wasn't humans I was interested in meeting!

Wading through the thick sawgrass swamps with only flashlight beams to light our way, tendrils of warm mist rising all around us, my wife, Tallulah, and I were on a mission.

Locals reported sighting strange colored spheres of light in the 'Glades. The idjits think they're created by marsh gases. We know better!

As far as *Cassandra's Guide to UFO's*—the UFO-hunter's holy bible!—tells it, they're Will-o'-the-Wisps! Diabolical death-dealing aliens!

If we get proof of their existence, it'll make our reps as celeb UFO-hunters!

Tallulah was first to see them! Three large balls of light——red, green, blue—— swooping and diving in the air ahead of us! Scouts from a mothership that must be high above, invisibly cloaked! The Bug-Eyes are sneaky that way!

I was about to snap off some pics when I noticed Tallulah moving slowly toward the lights, as if in a trance!

About to grab the foolish woman, my foot snagged on a root, and I crashed heavily into the water! By the time I had pulled myself out of the sucking mud, Tallulah and the lights——were gone!

The authorities believe that Tallulah was pulled down into the swamp and drowned, but I know better! The aliens took her! Poor Tallulah!

CASSANDRA'S GUIDE TO U.F.O'S

LLB PUBLISHING INC.

WILL-O'-THE-WISP FACT FILE

Location: The world
Appearance: Small glowing balls of colored light
Strength: Zilch!
Weaknesses: Shut your eyes and they can't hypnotize you! (O' course, you'll probably still fall into a swamp and drown, but hey, them's the breaks!)
Powers: Flight, levitation, teleportation, possible hypnosis
Fear Factor: 26 (Unless they really are aliens and they take you back to their home planet to experiment on! In which case Fear Factor: 5,000!!)

COOL USE FOR A WILL-O'-THE-WISP

Disco lights for your next hardcore party!

Fillet of a fenny snake,
In the cauldron boil and bake,
Eye of newt and toe of frog,
Wool of bat and tongue of dog,
Adder's fork and blind worm's sting,
Lizard's leg and howlet's wing,
For a charm of powerful trouble,
Like a hell-broth boil and bubble.

Double, double, toil and trouble;
Fire burn, and cauldron bubble.

Macbeth: Act 4, Scene 1

Truth? We find the works of ole Willy Shakespeare a total snooze-fest, but you have to give the dude credit. He writes one heck of a witches' chant!

Major shocker: Originally, witches only practiced their magic powers—for good! (And many totally rad White Witches still do!)

For thousands of years, witches (both women and men) used their amazing encyclopedic knowledge of nature to help people suffering from injury or illness, and to help ease the pain of childbirth. They were, in effect, the world's first homeopathic doctors! Respect!

(Medical note: Homeopathy uses natural substances such as plants, herbs, and minerals to help a patient rather than prescribing them pharmaceutical drugs.)

The word *witch* comes from the Old English words *wicca* (wizard) and *wicce* (sorceress), meaning both "wise" and "magic user."

You'd think people would be glad to have these in-the-know practitioners around to assist them.

Heck no! From AD 700 onward, the leaders who ran the Christian and Islamic religions took offense at witches healing their followers—they felt it was their job to do so through the simple power of prayer.

Since most witches did not follow the orthodox (established) religions, they were accused of heresy. (A heretic is someone who has an opinion or belief at odds with accepted beliefs or customs.)

To be a heretic meant—death!

Vicious lies, rumors, and misinformation spread like wildfire about witches putting a death-curse on their enemies, performing human sacrifice, and being in league with old pitchfork-wielding Satan himself!

This madness kicked off wholesale in the early fourteenth century. One could be accused of being a witch simply by looking at a neighbor "in a funny way"! (Serious!)

And if you were found guilty, you got tortured, flogged, tied to a stake, and—burned alive! (That and other equally gruesome deaths!)

The first recorded witch-burning took place in Kilkenny, Ireland, in 1324. Dame Alice Kyteler and her servant Petronilla de Meath were accused of sorcery and demonism. Dame Alice ran off to England, leaving poor Petronilla to her grisly fate!

This opened the floodgates to thousands of innocent people being hideously mutilated and murdered across the globe, most notably in Europe and North America!

So no wonder some witches decided to turn to the Dark Side!

Witches fly by their own power, or on brooms or rakes, or astride magical animals. They can also shape-change, preferring the form of a black cat!

If you upset these vengeful sorcerers or sorceresses, they'll call on the forces of evil to kill you in rather unpleasant ways, including zapping you with the Evil Eye (putting a curse on you from which there is no escape!), possessing your mind, murdering you in your sleep, and, of course, turning you into a toad! Radical!

Case Study 339/35W

Magic and the supernatural is a multibillion dollar industry! The delicious fright-night of Halloween is the second most popular (and profitable!) festival after Christmas, especially in the USA and Britain!

So for those of you who fancy transmogrifying (changing) into a witch for the weekend, here's an extract from a guide to modern witchcraft by celeb spell-caster Belladonna Foxglove . . . ! (To be read in a dry, cackly voice!)

Witches 101

You will need:

Pointy black hat or wand to channel thy inner magicks! (What? Ye thought witches only wore pointy hats as the latest fashion accessory? Get real, dearies! [Cackle!])

Flying broomstick. (Or vacuum cleaner for all ye modern witches out there!)

Black cat (familiar)

Book of spells

Cast-iron cauldron with which to mix thy bubbling potions!

Fresh flowers and herbs. (Aside from use in potions, they pleasantly fragrance thy witch's den! With all that blood, rotting animal body parts, and stinky excrement flying about, ye'll need it!)

Gemstones, crystals, magick talismans, and amulets to enhance the strength of thy magick and to direct at thy enemy!

Salt. Poured in a Circle of Protection in which ye stand to stop any demons ye call up by mistake from killing ye!

Have fun, dearies! (Cackle!)

(EVIL) WITCH FACT FILE

Location: The Multiverse!
Appearance: Hideous old hag with green skin and a gross, pus-filled, warty face
Strength: Devilish!
Weaknesses: A witch bottle. Take a strand of hair or an eyelash from a witch (without getting caught!) and place it in a small glass bottle alongside nine bent pins, some wool fibers, the leaves of prickly grass, and a squirt of your own urine. Bury the bottle under a warm open fireplace. Every time the witch tries to pass near water of any kind, she will then suffer terrible torments and eventually—death!
Powers: Everything, really! All they have to do is weave a spell, and—Poof! You're toast!
Fear Factor: 99.8

CATCH A WITCH AND . . .

Employ her as a lunch lady at your school for more "exotic" meals! (If bat's eyeballs and viper's tongue rattle your cage, that is! Hey, it can't be any worse than the stinking gloop your school already serves you!)

YUKI-ONNA (雪女)

1 ¥250

雪女
Yuki-Onna

comi

We've said it before: The freaking terrifying, to-the-max, deranged, femme-fatale (French for "fatal woman") flying fiends outclass many of their male counterparts, and here's a Japanese *yōkai* (spirit) to send chills down your spine . . . !

The death-dealing Yuki-Onna ("snow woman") haunts the mountain passes and forests of Japan's frozen north, including the areas of Osore-zan (Mountain of Terror!) and the Oga Peninsula, home to the Namahage mountain demons and also its awesomely spectacular naturally shaped *Godzilla* cliff formation! (Check it out!)

Appearing during winter, specifically January 1 to February 1 (although some *yōkai* experts claim they appear only during a full moon or fresh fall of snow), these vampiric ghosts were once women who died during snowstorms, and have returned to exact revenge.

With unnaturally pale skin, Yuki-Onna possesses an ethereal yet stunning beauty.

Extremely willowy and tall, up to ten feet in height, with long, flowing black hair, crimson eyes, and ice-blue lips, she wears a diaphanous (light and transparent) white kimono—or else rises up from the snow totally *naked*! (No wonder her lips are blue! Sheesh!)

Those who survive an encounter with Yuki-Onna claim that she levitates, flying with the grace of a gentle winter's breeze. And walks so softly upon the snow, she leaves no footprints. Or, like many other Japanese *yōkai*, has no feet at all!

A ruthless killing machine, Yuki-Onna takes great delight in offing people in a variety of beyond-nasty ways.

Breathing out glacial breath, she death-freezes her victims where they stand, their heart encased in thick ice!

Or, by a simple touch, roots them to the spot before kissing their lips and sucking out both their life force and their very soul, leaving behind an empty frozen husk to shatter into ice shards in the snow!

Favorite prey of Yuki-Onna are kids. Feet frozen by the demoness, horrified parents are forced to helplessly watch as Yuki-Onna drains the life outta their much-loved offspring! Brutal!

Often impatient for the kill, Yuki-Onna will simply break into a home and solidify everyone inside! Chillin'!

If you're going hunting for these lugubrious (profoundly melancholy) ladies, watch out for some neat if downright dirty tricks.

When threatened, a Yuki-Onna will shape-change into a thick mist or blizzard to blind her attacker, leading them off the edge of a mountain! Oooh, c-c-cold!

Case Study 786/5YO

Comics are big business! How so? In 2014, a copy of *Action Comics #1* (1938—the first appearance of Superman) sold for an eye-popping $3,207,852!! (Yep, that's three MILLION dollars! Wowsers!)

Other biggies include *Amazing Fantasy #15* (1962—the first appearance of Spider-Man) at $1,100,000 and *Detective Comics #27* (1939—the first appearance of Batman) at $1,075,000!

But if you think comics are popular in the West, they're nothing compared to sales of Japanese manga comics, some titles of which sell millions of copies each week! (FYI: "manga" in kanji [漫画]—Japanese script—means cartoon pictures, i.e., comics!)

Here's a recent news item from the American comics news site *Comic Book Round-Up* about the shocking death of a popular manga artist. The creator had just completed the first issue of his fantasy comic starring a Yuki-Onna!

August 16, Tokyo

According to Sumo Jujitsu, managing editor of the Mangarific Comics Company, one of Japan's most successful manga publishers, fan-favorite artist Kendo Aikido was found dead at his home yesterday.

Police report that 38-year-old Aikido, winner of numerous fandom awards for his quality Japanese horror comics, had mysteriously frozen to death, even though Japan is currently experiencing a freakish summer heat wave with temperatures reaching 98°F.

A spokesman for the Tokyo CSI (Crime Scene Investigation) unit said that Aikido had died of extreme hypothermia. "To be honest, it doesn't make much sense," she told reporters.

"A human's body temperature is constantly maintained at around 97.7–99.5°F. Severe hypothermia—a condition where your body temperature drops to dangerously low levels—can kill if it reaches 86°F.

"Aikido's body temperature was *minus* 273.15°F. In other words, Absolute Zero. His body literally froze solid, which is scientifically impossible!"

Comic fandom is in shock over Aikido's sudden death. His latest work, a series based on the murderous Japanese ghost Yuki-Onna, was released only this week.

Some fans on social network sites have claimed that a real Yuki-Onna took offense at Aikido's portrayal of her and paid him a less-than-friendly visit to complain!

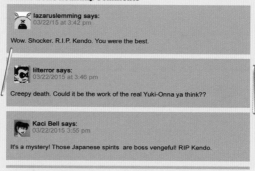

📄 Filed under: Comics, Top News   ⬤ Tagged with: Kendo Aikido, Yuki-Onna, Comics

Comic News Roundup Comments

lazaruslemming says:
03/22/15 at 3:42 pm

Wow. Shocker. R.I.P. Kendo. You were the best.

lilterror says:
03/22/2015 at 3:46 pm

Creepy death. Could it be the work of the real Yuki-Onna ya think??

Kaci Bell says:
03/22/2015 3:55 pm

It's a mystery! Those Japanese spirits are boss vengeful! RIP Kendo.

YUKI-ONNA FACT FILE

Location: Forests and mountains, northern Japan
Appearance: Impressively tall, beautiful young woman with long black (sometimes pure white) hair, red eyes, and ice-blue lips
Strength: Frigid!
Weaknesses: Water! Cold water swells her up to blimp size; hot water melts her!
Powers: Weather control, shape-shifting (thick mist, snowstorm, frozen puddle of water), vampiric soul-sucker!
Fear Factor: 42

WHAT TO DO WITH A CAPTURED YUKI-ONNA

Use her powers to replenish the melting Antarctic ice shelf, which is breaking apart at a terrifying rate thanks to accelerated climate change (which is caused by moronic humanity's unthinking pollution and destruction of our planet!)
Or else tell her to create an ice skating rink in your backyard, and charge your pals to use it! (Heck, we can be just as mercenary as the next dude!)

FLYING FIENDS FACT FILES

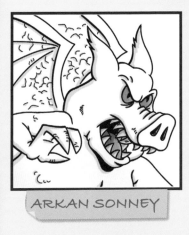

ARKAN SONNEY

Location: The Isle of Man, UK (Travel note: The island is located in the Irish Sea between Great Britain and Ireland. Capital city—Douglas [pronounced "Doolish"]. Size—thirty-three miles long, thirteen miles wide. Population—85,300. Language—English, Manx [a Celtic language originating on the Isle of Man]. The island is a monster hunter's delight, awash with fairies, brownies—and giants!)

Appearance: Fairy winged pig creature, very elusive and hard to catch. White with red eyes and red prickly ears.

Strength: The magical piggy kind!

Weaknesses: Mud baths!

Powers: Size-changer—body swells to enormous proportions! Brings fortune and good luck. (If you catch one, you'll magically find a silver piece in your pocket!)

Fear Factor: Tch, get real! It's a cute widdle piggy! Minus 1000!

DIRAE

Location: Greece

Appearance: These ladies are Da Bomb! They're close cousins to the equally petrifying Greek demons the Erinyes (aka the Roman Furies). Head of a dog! Hair made from live snakes! Snakes also entwine their arms! They have jet-black skin and giant bat wings! Noxious!

Strength: They're deities, dude! You know, GODS of the Underworld!

Weaknesses: Anyone who survives an encounter with these bestial beauties deserves respect! They are all-powerful!! (Well, apart from their gag-inducing stinky breath, that is!)

Powers: Dirae bring down terrifying vengeance upon kids who talk back to their parents and teachers, bullies who pick on the weak, hosts who are rude to their guests, miserable or noisy neighbors, litter-droppers, politicians, bank managers, real estate agents, cold-call salespeople . . . you know, all the really annoying people of the world! The Dirae haunt their victims incessantly until they die in screaming torment! Righteous!

Fear Factor: 91.9

FLYING HEAD

Location: The forests of North America and Canada where the Iroquois tribe lives. (Cultural note: The Iroquois, pronounced Eer-uh-kwoy, or in their own tongue, *Goano'ganoch'sa'jeh'seroni* [go on, we double-dare you to pronounce that!], is a Six Nation [*Haudenosaunee*] Confederacy made up of the Mohawk, Seneca, Oneida, Onondaga, Cayuga, and Tuscarora tribes. Population—approx. 125,000.)

Appearance: Terrifying gigantic human head (called *Kanontsistóntie's*), which is taller than a man! This primordial monstrosity has long, black, matted hair; demonic eyes; huge jagged teeth; clawed talons; and bat wings for ears! (Cool!)

Strength: Can carry off cattle between its teeth!

Weaknesses: Hot acorns! (So make sure you pack a good supply on your hunt!)

Powers: Creates whirlwinds. Swoops down on stormy nights to snatch up cattle or children and take them away to snack on while watching its favorite horror films—its idea of cartoons!

Fear Factor: For Iroquois kids and moo-cows—99.9!

FUXI

Location: Mountain regions of China & Japan

Appearance: Head of a man, body of a large rooster! (Yup, we go from the sublime to the snort-choking ridiculous in this book! Nothing stops us!)

Strength: *Psst!* Word up! It's not its puny rooster-type strength you should be worrying about! Read on!

Weaknesses: Hates peace and happiness in the world. So . . .

Powers: The Fuxi is the dark omen—of WAR! Sight a Fuxi, and wholesale death and destruction is imminent! Considering the number of completely unnecessary and mindless wars stupid politicians worldwide like to start up on a yearly basis, ole Fuxi is doing an excellent job!

Fear Factor: 93.4

Location: Austria and Germany
Appearance: Three-legged vampiric bird with a goat face
Strength: Mondo-ferocious!
Weaknesses: Can't resist gulping down the pumping warm blood of cattle in the fields! While it's doing so, sneak up behind it, swinging your cold-iron sword, and—SHUNK! Off with its head!
Powers: Super-fast speed due to its three legs. Much like the Banshee, the Habergeiss cries out a haunting moan at night to indicate a death, especially that of a child!
Fear Factor: 53.4

HABERGEISS

Location: Mountains and forests of Albania (small country in the Balkans in southeastern Europe. Albania neighbors—Greece, Macedonia, Kosovo, and Montenegro. Size—11,100 square miles. Capital city—Tiranë. Population—3,162,000.)
Appearance: Horned, spiny, fire-breathing dragon with nine tongues; or an enormous woman with an extremely hairy body! (For the first twelve years of its life cycle it is a smaller serpent or dragon known as the Bolla.)
Strength: Big dragon-y kind.
Weaknesses: Human sacrifice. (Of course, first you have to convince some dope to lie half naked on a stone altar with his eyes closed while you hold a sharp dagger above his chest! "Trust me," you tell him. "This won't hurt me one little bit!")
Powers: Shape-shifting. Spits fire from its body that dries out a town's water supply!
Fear Factor: 37

KULSHEDRA

NASHNAS

Location: Republic of Yemen, a country situated at the southwest tip of the Arabian Peninsula on the Red Sea opposite Ethiopia. To the north is Saudi Arabia, to the east, Oman. (Size— 203,849 square miles. Capital city—Sana'a. Population—23,852,400. Language— Arabic.)

Appearance: Evil Jinn (aka Djinn) born from a human and a Shiqq (a lower form of Jinn). Half a human body split vertically with one arm, one leg, and half a head. Bat wings. Some may be missing head and neck and have their faces on their chests.

Strength: Demonic, because they're like, well, demons!

Weaknesses: Cold iron!

Powers: Shape-shifting. Demonic magic. Weather control.

Fear Factor: 66.5

NGANI-VATU

Location: The 333 volcanic and coral islands and more than 500 islets that are part of the nation of Fiji in the tropical South Pacific Ocean. Capital city—Suva, on the main island of Viti Levu. Population—874,750 spread across the 110 inhabited islands. Language—English, Fijian, Fiji Hindi.

Appearance: Gigantic predatory bird, so big that its vast body eclipses the sun! You heard us—the SUN!! (Once caught, you're going to need a very BIG birdcage to keep it in!)

Strength: Humongous, we'd imagine!

Weaknesses: No idea! Any suggestions?

Powers: Its mighty beating wings create hurricane-strength storms! Super-fast speed. Swooping down, it snatches up helpless humans in its huge talons to take back to its nest to feast on!

Fear Factor: 48.8

PIHUECHENYI

Location: The Araucanía (aka Araucana) region of Chile, South America. The Pihuechenyi targets the Mapuche, who make up 80 percent of the indigenous peoples in Chile, or 9 percent of the total population.

Appearance: Winged vampire snake

Strength: It's no giant boa constrictor.

Weaknesses: As one of the Undead, it is susceptible to the usual: wooden stake, silver cross/bullet/dagger, garlic, beheading, and other cool anti-vamp tricks!

Powers: Intangibility (able to pass through solid objects). Invisibility. Attacks when its victim is asleep. (Coward!)

Fear Factor: 26.9

SUANGGI

Location: Maluku Islands, Indonesia, Southeast Asia. There are approximately 1,027 islands, the largest two being Halmahera and Seram. Capital city—Ambon, on one of the small islands, which, confusingly, is also called . . . Ambon! Population of islands—approx. two million. (Population of the whole of Indonesia? 246,864,191! Well, it was the last time we counted!)

Appearance: In the daytime, an ordinary female human with bleary, red eyes. At night, the head detaches (along with all the inner bits—lungs, diaphragm, heart, kidneys, intestines, bladder, etc., which then hang down from it. Nice.) and flies through the air looking for victims.

Strength: Crazy cannibal sorceress—as strong as she wants to be!

Weaknesses: Lots and lots of—PRAYERS!! They won't kill a Suanggi, but she'll (probably) keep away!

Powers: Immortality. (Suanggis are born from Suanggi parents, generation to generation.) Sickness-giver. The slightest touch from these female freakazoids, and you've had it! You fall ill and die slowly, the Suanggis gathering around your house waiting for your death so that they can feast on your liver! (Their favorite snack!)

Fear Factor: 74.6

VETALA

Location: Bit weird this: they live in stones scattered on the hills both inside and outside of cemeteries in India. (Like you do!)

Appearance: Demonic, vampiric wraith-spirits. Humans turned zombie-fied by Vetala (see below) have their hands and feet pointing backward. (Neat trick, but kinda gross!) They're ticked-off souls trapped between this world and the next because the proper funeral rites were not performed on them.

Strength: As strong as the zombie corpse they control.

Weaknesses: Give them the proper funeral rites, and they're gone! A nice gift will make them leave you alone! Counter-spells!

Powers: Sorcery. Necromancy (raising the dead to predict the future and to acquire great knowledge).

Vetalas enter fresh corpses in cemeteries to bring them back to Un-Life. (They reside in these corpses during the day, leaving them at night to feed on the living, especially kids! While possessed, the corpse does not decay, thus saving on the purchase of super-strength wrinkle-cream products!)

If a Vetala inhabits the living, it causes miscarriages in pregnant women and freaked-out insanity in anyone else! They are a font of intel on all things past, present, and future! (So if you catch one, force it to give you next week's winning lottery numbers!)

Fear Factor: 61.9

WYVERN

Location: The world! (That about covers it!)

Appearance: Li'l bro to the dragons. Fierce serpent head and body, bat wings, only two legs (most dragons have four), barbed tail.

Strength: Ferociously strong

Weaknesses: Cannot breathe fire. Mondo-clumsy—always tripping over its own feet. Kinda stoopid. A good sword thrust to the heart should take one down.

Powers: Poisoned breath, poisoned tail stinger. Wyverns encourage and spread envy, greed, mistrust, plague, and war. (So, absolutely no different from most politicians and journalists, then! Just sayin'!)

Fear Factor: 42

GRUESOME CREATURES

Searchers after horror haunt strange, far places.

—Howard Phillips (H.P.) Lovecraft (1890–1937),

American horror writer

If you thought the gnarly Flying Fiends were horrific, wait until you get a load of this veritable grab bag of the most psychotic, flesh-rendering, intestine-chomping, eyeball-sucking, abominable abominations that take delicious pleasure in hunting down their favorite prey: humans!

This section covers them all! Vampires, zombies, zombie-vampires, ghastly ghosts, grisly ghouls, gross gremlins, hair-raising animal horrors, and hideous water beasts! These are many of the *most deadly* supernatural devils out there!

So make sure your passport is up-to-date, because you're going to be traveling across the globe in your never-ending quest to hunt them down!

And while you're at it, download the latest language apps. You won't get far if you can't speak the local lingo!

Want to know the top-ten most-spoken languages? We guarantee you're going to be surprised! If you think English is the numero-uno language, you need double geography studies! It's not even the *second* most-spoken language!

Mandarin Chinese tops the charts with 848 million speakers, more than double that of the 406 million people who speak Spanish. So where's English, you ask? An embarrassing third place with a paltry 335 million!

Then there's Hindi (260 million), Arabic (223 million), Portuguese (202 million), Bengali

(193 million), Russian (162 million), Japanese (122 million), and Javanese, which is spoken in Indonesia (84.3 million). German and French don't even rank!

(Culture note: If you want to hear many different languages in the same place, hop on a plane to London, England! Over 300—yes, *300!*—different languages are spoken there, more than in any other city in the world! Wowsers!)

And here are some of the merciless, malignant monstrosities you'll clash with on your travels!

In the UK, prepare to battle the invisible Alp-Luachra, deadly Unseelie fairies who eat you alive—from the inside! Sweet!

Speaking of eating you, the Australian Yara-Ma-Yha-Who goes one better and swallows you whole!

That worldwide nocturnal, nightmarish, demonic Sandman will make you gouge out your own eyes! While the Brazilian brute the Headless Mule sucks out your eyeballs before trampling you to death! Neat!

Another equine-featured creepoid is the Greek hellion of the Underworld, Empousa, who literally feasts on your bones!

Watch your back in Africa, because the leopard-troll Ga-Gorib gets his kicks by stoning you to death! The Japanese Teke-Teke prefers cutting you in half with her bloody scythe, and the Native American demon baby Raw Gums strangles and eats his victims and has the even-neater trick of calling the dead back to Unlife! Apocalyptic!

Don't forget to bring us back a souvenir of your travels . . . that is, if you actually survive the trip!

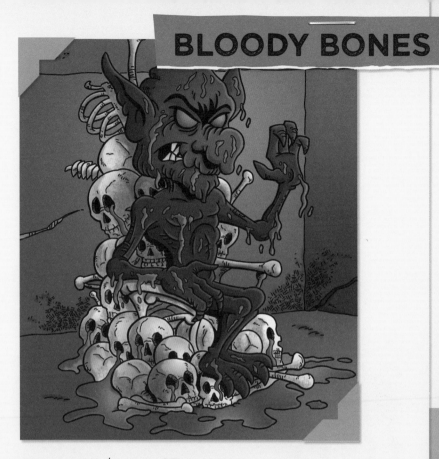

BLOODY BONES

You want gruesome? You're going to GET gruesome!

We're starting off with the grossest, sickest, most repulsive and twisted demonic homicidal maniac child-killer ever to hack a grisly blood-splattered path through the cowering throng of humanity!

(Anyone suffering from hemophobia, the fear of blood, BEWARE—this chapter's only for the hardest of hardcore monster hunters!)

Known under a variety of monikers (names), including Rawhead, Tommy Rawhead, Tommy Rawhead and Bloody Bones (yep, all one tag!), or simply Bloody Bones, this apparently immortal horror's origins are lost to the opaque mists of time.

Some say he first appeared in Africa at the very dawn of true humanity.

Others argue that he is of Celtic descent, and was eagerly awaiting the arrival of the earliest settlers to Ireland between 8000 and 7000 BC, his prized collection of filleting knives honed razor sharp in preparation for slowly, agonizingly slicing the fresh tender skin from the bodies of screaming, terrified Stone Age kids!

He now performs his hematic (bloody) gore-fests in England (specifically Lancashire and Yorkshire), Ireland, and the southern United States!

The dude is first referred to in the anti-Catholic short story "Wyll of the Deuyll" ("Will of the Devil," pub. 1548), written by celeb Elizabethan poet George Gascoigne (1535–1577), wherein Bloody Bones is described as the Devil's faithful secretary in the Court of Hell!

A shape-shifter par excellence (French for "by excellence," i.e., the very best), BB can appear as a hobgoblin, dwarf, or gremlin, with wrinkly, scab-encrusted skin. Or of human shape with fourth-degree burns over his entire body—perhaps an old man or dog, the flesh hideously scarred. And in America as a huge, upright-standing zombie razorback hog!

(Medical note: Our bodies contain 62,000 miles of blood vessels—yep, we counted each and every one! Red cells make up 40 percent of our blood's volume. And there are around five million of them in a single drop of blood!)

One place Bloody Bones can be found hanging out is near ponds and wells, or inside street drains, waiting to pull in naughty kids and drown them!

But his favorite spot is INSIDE your house! Especially in cupboards or under the stairs, or down in the dank, dark basement!

To see him you need only to bend forward and peek between your legs. He'll be seated proudly on a throne of children's skulls and bones, blood pouring from his head, cackling dementedly!

If you're in the habit of swearing or lying, he'll pull you in and FLAY YOU ALIVE!!! (And, obviously, EAT YOU!!!)

Case Study 613/6BB

Let's face it, "reality" TV shows are totally lame. Especially the ones where a bunch of publicity-seeking people sit around a house for weeks on end inanely arguing with one another.

Equally dumb? So-called "talent" shows!

But the ones we hate most? Home-makeover shows! Can you believe millions of people worldwide actually waste their precious lives watching this garbage? Unbelievable!

Here's an excerpt from the transcript of the popular midmorning makeover show *Wrecking Rooms*, featuring the saccharine, vomit-inducing presenters Colin and Lucille! (FYI: A film or TV "script" includes all of the locations, action, and dialogue. A "transcript" consists only of the dialogue.)

COLIN

Heck, when that family returns and sees what color
we've painted their walls, they're gonna freak!

LUCILLE

Sure will, Col. They wanted something different,
and you can't beat plaid for a modern style statement!

COLIN

For sure. Now let's see about making over this
basement. Oh, blast. No light. Bulb must've popped.

LUCILLE

You'd think the birdbrains would make
sure of these things before we got here.

COLIN

Um, Lucille, going out *live*, remember?

LUCILLE

Oops. Only kidding, folks. They're a great family. Honest.

COLIN

Watch your step, Luce. Something's crunching underfoot.
And, ew, what's this slimy goo down the handrail? Lights,
someone! Ah, better. Oh, man, look at this! Someone's spilled
red paint everywhere. Disgusting!

LUCILLE

Aw, jeez! What's that stench? Rotting carcass?

COLIN

Well, viewers, we hope your home's in better condition
than this! There are small bones scattered all over
the floor. Family must own a whole pack of dogs!

LUCILLE

Um, Col, I'm no expert, but this looks like a leg
bone. A . . . *human* leg bone! A . . . child's leg bone!

COLIN

OMG! You're right! Someone call the cops! No, wait!
Hear that? Like . . . soft cackling! Someone's down here!

LUCILLE

Col! Over there! A man . . . or . . . creature . . . sitting on
that chair! His head . . . bleeding . . . oh! Gross!

COLIN

Not a chair, Luce . . . a throne . . . a throne of . . . bones!
And . . . skulls! All that blood! Cameraman! Cut
transmission! Cut trans . . . *Ahhhhhhhh!*

The TV crew were never seen alive again!

BLOODY BONES FACT FILE

Location: England, Ireland, USA
Appearance: Dwarf dude covered in
blood and grody to the max!
Strength: Demonically supernatural
or supernaturally demonic—take your
pick!
Weaknesses: Um, anyone got a spare
nuke we could borrow?
Powers: Shape-shifting, immortality,
magic—he turns bad brats into trash
that their parents will then throw out!
Fear Factor: 92.9

CATCH BLOODY BONES AND . . .

Give him a list of the bullies at your
school! He'll soon deal with them!

The poor Mapuche folk of Chile are regularly terrorized by the GINORMOUS estiferous (producing heat) man-monster known as—Cherufe!

With a totally rad pumped-up body of magma-burning rock, this all-powerful extremophile lives deep within the bowels of Chile's two thousand volcanoes, more than five hundred of which are still potentially active!

(FYI: An extremophile is an organism that can survive mega-extreme conditions that would kill most other life-forms! The best example of this is the totally awesome—and awesomely cute!—1,500-plus species of tardigrade (aka Water Bear), miniscule 0.0020-inch water-dwelling creatures that live for up to two hundred years and can survive being dropped into scalding water of 303.8 degrees Fahrenheit, being chilled to a bone-shattering *minus* 458 degrees Fahrenheit, being zapped with one thousand times more deadly radiation than any other creature could possibly survive, and happily float around in the vacuum of space! Now *that's* extreme—to the max!)

Cherufe is a mondo, A1–quality shape-shifter who can morph his always GIGANTIC humanoid form into that of a fiery rock-man, a snake-headed man, a serpent with a ram's head, a bipedal lizard, a dragon, or any and all of the above!

This dude has got some seriously neat attack abilities, including snorting out freaking *fireballs* from his nostrils and transforming himself into a huge blazing meteor that he shoots skyward before smashing back down to earth to wipe out entire villages!

To appease Cherufe, he demands regular human sacrifice, preferably young virgin women, who are thrown alive into a volcano for Cherufe to feast upon!

Ripping off the heads of his victims, he sets them alight and kicks them shooting back out of the crater! The blazing skulls crash down upon the village, rolling on the ground before glaring up accusingly at their heartbroken families!

And if sacrifices are not made to him, an irate Cherufe simply erupts the volcano, destroying all! Apocalyptic!

Case Study 505/27C

For those of you who slept through history class, World War II (1939–1945) was kind of a big deal.

Over forty million people died because psycho megalomaniac (a person obsessed with power) fruitcake Adolf Hitler (1889–1945), Chancellor (leader) of

Nazi Germany and owner of the lamest moustache evvverrr, basically wanted to kill all those he hated (which was, like, everyone!) and take over the world.

Guess what! He failed! Ha! Looo-serrr!

Members of Hitler's totally evil military force, the Schutzstaffel (the SS; translated to "Protection Echelon") and the Gestapo (Geheime Staatspolizei, "Secret State Police"), who gleefully tortured and murdered tens of millions, ran away after the war to avoid having their necks stretched.

More than nine thousand Nazi war criminals hid out in South American countries, including between five hundred and one thousand in Chile.

During our extensive investigations, we came across secret documents that reveal a shocking secret!

SS-Grupenführer (Group Leader) Karl Teufel, one of the SS thugs hiding out in Chile, tried to enlist Cherufe to return the Nazis to power!

Here's a terrifying extract from the last of those files, written by Teufel's assistant! (Translated, natch!)

Puyehue, Chile

Date: Friday 13 September 1946
THE CHERUFE EXPERIMENT

ADDENDUM

In his madness, the Grupenführer had kidnapped a young virgin girl from the nearby village, dragging her at gunpoint up the shuddering flank of the 7,336-foot, active Puyehue volcano in the Puyehue National Park!

Molten rocks and thick streams of blistering hot lava reaching temperatures of 2,282 degrees Fahrenheit flowed from the crater, a thick ash plume choking us. I was certain the volcano was going to erupt at any moment!

"Dummkopf!" growled the Grupenführer upon seeing me hesitate. "Once we sacrifice this pathetic whelp to Cherufe, he will be ours to command! We shall use his infinite powers to crush our enemies and return the glory of the Third Reich!"

Reaching the lip and ignoring the pain of our shoes melting, Teufel looked down into the mouth of Hell itself!

"Cherufe! Come to me!" he screeched, peering into the scorching magma, sweat boiling on his face. "Your master bids you appear!"

Minutes passed like hours. Then, rising slowly from deep inside the one-and-a-half-mile-wide caldera, until it towered over us, blocking out the sun, was a sight most monstrous!

"Mein Gott!" gasped Teufel in admiration, looking up at the huge burning rock monster. "You are *prächtig*! Magnificent!"

He eagerly pushed forward the screaming girl. "Take this worthless creature as an offering!"

Cherufe reached down——toward the Grupenführer!

"Was im Himmel?!" What in Heaven?!" he cried. "No! No! Keep back! Keep . . . !"

The Cherufe's fist closed around Teufel, who screamed piteously as his clothes ignited, burning off his flesh to the bone!

With a mighty roar, Cherufe tore the head from Teufel's neck and swallowed it whole, before spitting it out again, a flaming skull!

The girl and I ran! And ran! The Grüpenfuhrer's mad dream of returning the Third Reich to greatness has ended in ashes——as has he!

CHERUFE FACT FILE

Location: Volcanoes of Chile, South America
Appearance: Magma-scorching giant rock-monster, but changes appearance to suit his moods.
Strength: A wimp!
Weaknesses: Giant ice sword! Stab it through Cherufe's chest before it melts! (Difficulty level: 10,000+!!)
Powers: Shape-shifting, creates deadly volcanic eruptions, exploding fiery meteor ability, snorts out fireball snot, eats virgins!
Fear Factor: 99.9

WHAT TO DO WITH CHERUFE

Use him to heat your swimming pool in winter——and be ready to run if he catches a cold and starts sneezing!

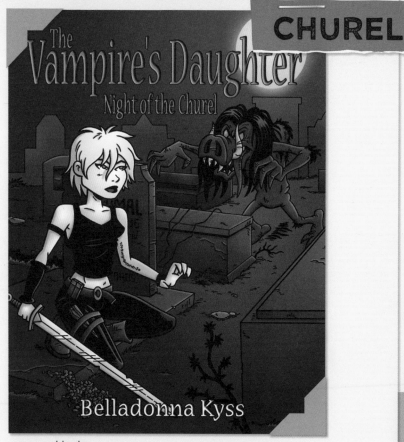

The Vampire's Daughter
Night of the Churel

Belladonna Kyss

Vampires exist—worldwide!

They are especially prevalent in India, the country from which many vampirologists (those who study and hunt vampires) believe they first originated.

Arguably, India's first vampire was the death-dealing Hindu goddess Kali! (*Kali* is the female form of the word *kalam*, meaning "black" or "dark-colored.")

She of the atrous (jet-black) skin, protruding fangs, elongated black tongue dripping blood, and four arms!

Sporting a fashionable skirt made from human arms and hands, and a necklace of fifty-two shrunken heads, she brandishes a bloody scimitar (sword with curved blade) while holding up the severed head of one of her victims! Brutal!

Another gang of South Asian female revenants (Undead ghouls) we don't look forward to meeting without our bag of nifty apotropaic (designed to stop evil) tricks are the vampire ghosts who nightly haunt the shadowy streets and alleyways of North India, Bangladesh, and Pakistan—the Churel!

First off, don't let their appearance as beautiful young women with warm, wholesome smiles fool ya.

Their *true* shape is utterly foul and repugnant! The Churel have demonic or boarlike visages with fangs or tusks, lank filthy hair, long black tongues, jutting teeth, thick ugly lips, and blood-splattered clawlike hands, and are often hunchbacked with backward-facing feet! And some Churels have no mouth at all!

MAGIC MIRROR ON THE WALL, WHO IS THE FAIREST ONE OF ALL?

WITH APOLOGIES TO THE BROTHERS GRIMM

They are the vengeful spirits of women who were either treated badly by their family when alive, or who died during childbirth, usually during the annual Hindu Diwali festival.

(FYI: Diwali—a shortened version of the word "Dipavali"—literally means "rows of lighted lamps," aka "festival of lights." Diwali falls on the fifteenth day of the Hindu month of Kartika, during October or November. This colorful, fun festival lasts five days, the fourth day of Diwali being the Hindu New Year.)

Rather peeved at dying during such a stonking cool festival, a Churel at first targets the male relatives of her family, starting with either her husband or the most cherished member (obviously the youngest) and then working her way through the rest of her menfolk until none are left alive!

Her bloodlust never satisfied, she then starts on male friends and neighbors for good measure!

Using hypnotic powers to entice her prey into her clutches, she proceeds to drink his blood and steal his life force until his body is left a withered, brittle husk, old before its time!

Case Study 003/41C

Literary note: Carmilla, an amazeballs story about the world's first fictional female vampire, was published way back in 1872 by Irish author Joseph Sheridan Le Fanu (1814–1873), predating Bram Stoker's Dracula by twenty-five years!

Nowadays, Urban Fantasy is a popular fiction genre (category) that mixes fantasy and urban elements.

A recent UF publisher ran into legal trouble when he produced The Vampire's Daughter, a series of novels based on the real-life exploits of vampire hunter Karmilla Darkskye, who is a Dhampir (half vampire, half human!).

Personally, we think her own diary entries are much more thrilling!

October 26/15th day of Kartika——Bangalore, India

The evening streets of the city are thronged with people celebrating Diwali, rapturous joy on their faces.

I alone sit in the ancient cemetery of colorful gravestones topped with lingams (symbols) that represent the Hindu deity Shiva, and Nandi bulls.

The entire cemetery is covered in trash; cows, goats, and packs of wild dogs roam between the graves.

I patiently await an appearance by a Churel, one I've been tracking this past week. Already, she has had murderous vengeance upon three male members of her family, the youngest being only seven.

In her twisted mind, she blames them for her death one year past.

The city-center clock strikes the midnight hour. From the woman's burial plot, wisps of ethereal mist rise up, transforming into a hideous creature with a visage that is half boar, half demon, feet abnormally twisted.

"So, Dhampir, your father informed me of your presence," the foul figure sibilantly hisses upon seeing me. "And to him I have promised——your death!"

With a hell-born shriek, she lunges! Ducking beneath her savage attack, her claws painfully raking my face, I withdraw my sword, Seraph!

Viciously, I slice at the Churel, the blade passing harmlessly through her intangible body!

"Foolish child! You cannot harm a ghost!" cackles the demented spirit. "But I can suck the very life force from you!"

She launches herself at me once more, fangs glistening in the moonlight!

I pull from my pocket a small pouch, emptying the contents onto the ground!

"Nooo!" howls the enraged vampiric ghoul, leaping greedily upon the hundreds of tiny mustard seeds. "You have discovered—my one weakness!"

Losing interest in me, she begins intently picking up the seeds, one by one!

Acting swiftly, I incant a spell that pulls her, screaming helplessly, back into her grave forevermore!

CHUREL FACT FILE

Location: North India, Bangladesh, and Pakistan—in South Asia

Appearance: Boar/demon with fang/tusk-clawed-hunchback combo!

Strength: Incorporeal—you can't hit it!

Weaknesses: If you are able to get to one while it's still a fresh corpse, drive a few nails through its hands and feet, and put iron chains or rings around the feet and burning red peppers over the eyes! Snap the legs above the ankles, twist the feet backward, and tie the big toes together! If facing a Churel, cover the ground with mustard seeds—they find them irresistible! Then zap her with an exorcism!

Powers: Shape-shifting, hypnotism

Fear Factor: 88

HOW TO CATCH CHUREL

Trick her into turning into a mist and suck her up inside an industrial-strength vacuum cleaner!

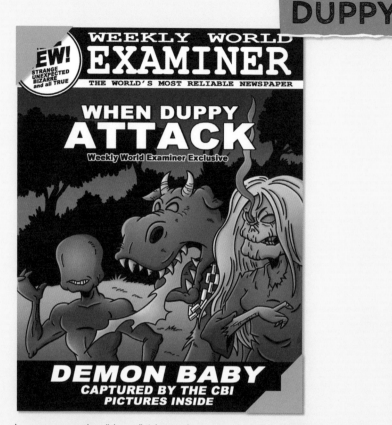

Much like the Japanese *yōkai*, "duppy" (aka jumbee or jumbie) is the collective name for all sorts of gnarly ghouls, soul-stealing spirits, dank monsters, and warped apparitions that haunt, hunt, and munch on humans across the seven thousand–plus islands of the glorious sun-drenched Caribbean!

A duppy is the soul of a dead person. This soul remains linked to its place of death. To confuse the duppy into traveling to the afterlife, the deceased's family will rearrange their furniture so the duppy won't recognize its former home.

We thought you'd like a quick checklist of some of the more thugish boogers you're liable to run into while dipping your toes in the warm Caribbean Sea!!

A duppy can be a ghost or spirit with an amorphous (formless) shadow-dark body. When it touches someone, he barfs violently and incessantly until he eventually dies!

(Culinary side note: Parmesan cheese—aka Parmigiano-Reggiano—contains butyric acid, which is also found in stinky body odor and puke and poo! Delish!)

Then there's the child-stealing Douens, rotted souls of little munchkins who died before they were baptized and are trapped on Earth forevermore.

Located in deep forests and near rivers, they appear as an epicene (lacking characteristics of either sex) naked child with a blank face (except for a mouth slit) and backward-facing feet. They lead kids away from their homes and lose them deep in the forest, never again to be seen!

And how about the Rollin' Calf? This sometimes fire-breathing mammalian monstrosity is easily recognized by the fiery red eyes and thick chain wrapped around its neck!

Two demonic damsel duppies include Ol' Higue (aka Old Suck), a witch-crone who feeds on sleeping villagers by sucking all the breath from them! And La Diablesse (aka Lajables), the Devil Woman, she of the corpse face and eyes of burning coals and the Devil's cloven feet! She entices young men away from their village before losing them in the forest, where they will eventually fall into a river and drown or be eaten alive by wild hogs! Righteous!

Case Study 383/11D

Neela Nightshade, ace reporter for the Weekly World Examiner, filed this horrifying story about multiple deaths in the Caribbean!

WHEN DUPPY ATTACK

Weekly World Examiner Exclusive

RIVERTON CITY, Kingston, Jamaica,
June 2

This luxurious Caribbean island is justifiably recognized for its unparalleled beauty, stunning vistas, and warm summer temperatures that regularly max at 90 degrees Fahrenheit.

It is also a country with high levels of violent crime, abject poverty, homelessness (hidden from the eyes of wealthy western tourists, naturally), and——DEMONIC MURDERS!

Such as I have discovered in Riverton City, a place so foul, death itself is an almost welcome relief!

In this rundown area of Kingston, capital city of Jamaica, in the sweltering heat, dust, dirt, and noise, more than five thousand people live in decrepit one-room tin shacks beside the island's largest garbage dump.

There is no plumbing or indoor toilet facilities, and no clean water to drink. Of all the many Hells on Earth, this must rank in my top ten.

In the past month, nine people have been killed or have completely vanished. Men, women——and kids! The bodies found have either been burned or were somehow asphyxiated, their breath literally sucked from their bodies!

"Duppy," comes the whispered chants of terrified villagers. "Duppy! DUPPY!"

With help from a local wise man, I stand in the village at midnight, facing a cotton tree, and perform Obeah, a form of spiritual magic that should bring forth Duppy.

For protection, I wear my clothes inside out and stand in a circle of rice, looking through a keyhole as I wipe dog *yampee*——dried mucus from the animal's eyes——into *my* eye as the clock strikes twelve!

I am expecting the appearance of one duppy, but from the swirling supernatural miasma (terrible smelling gas) before me step forth three! A faceless child whose feet are hideously twisted, a cadaverous emaciated old crone with eyes of burning coals, and a fire-breathing cow!

"Foolish mortal!" hisses the woman as the trio silently approaches with grim intent. "To call up a duppy is——to DIE!"

"Not tonight!" I growl, pulling off my left shoe and turning it upside down on the ground. The duppy are now frozen, unable to move except by my direction!

I order them to stand together for a group shot, then toss handfuls of salt at them.

Powerless to resist, they fall to the ground, counting each and every grain until the sun comes up and they return, screeching, to the spirit world!

DUPPY FACT FILE

Location: The cotton trees of the Caribbean
Appearance: Take your pick!
Strength: Depends on the Duppy!
Weaknesses: Salt, unable to cross rivers, wearing your clothes inside out, swearing, scattering salt or rice around your house, taking off your left shoe and turning it upside down on the ground before walking away backward.
Powers: Shape-shifting, magic
Fear Factor: 58.4

HOW TO CATCH A DUPPY

Do you realize how many of these critters there are?! Hundreds! And hundreds of ways to catch them! So choose one and then RESEARCH it! (We can't do everything for you! Sheesh!)

SCARLETT

MAGAZINE MARCH/APRIL

first look!!!
175
spring trends

+
SPEED DATING
EXPOSED

EMPOUSA'S
Dating Secrets

scarlettmag.com

Demons come in all shapes and sizes, but you just gotta love one who sports a leg made of cow poo! Yes, *poo*! Mental!

Where's the proof that Empousa has a leg made of manure? Well, duh! Because it says so in Ancient Greek playwright Aristophanes' comic play *The Frogs*.

This play was first performed at the annual dramatic competition during the Lenaia, which was a festival of Dionysus, in Athens in 405 BC—and ol' Ari won first prize!

His story features hardcore Greek god and hero Dionysus taking a summer-vacation road trip to Hades (Hell) to bring the playwright Euripedes back from the dead.

He drags along with him his slave Xanthias, who's much tougher and vastly more intelligent than his dopey master.

Here's a cool scene from the play where the pair runs into the hideous demoness Empousa! (Trust us! You'll love it!)

> Xanthias: And now I see the most ferocious monster.
>
> Dionysus: O, what's it like?
>
> Xanthias: Like everything by turns. Now it's a bull; now it's a mule; and now the loveliest girl.
>
> Dionysus: O, where? I'll go and meet her.
>
> Xanthias: It's ceased to be a girl; it's a dog now.
>
> Dionysus: It is Empousa!
>
> Xanthias: Well, its face is all ablaze with fire.
>
> Dionysus: Has it a copper leg?
>
> Xanthias: A copper leg? Yes, one; and one of cow dung.
>
> Dionysus: O, whither shall I flee?
>
> Xanthias: O, whither I?

There's no arguing with a story like that!

Some experts claim that the Empusai (plural of) are shape-shifting hellions of the Underworld, the daughters of the goddess Hecate and the spirit Mormo.

They are variously described as having donkeylike features, or of a dog or ox, with flaming red hair, one leg copper or brass, and the other that of a mule or made of cow poo!

An alternate theory argues that they're vengeful flying ghosts who merely work for the demon queen Hecate, appearing as an old hag monster with snakelike hair and a flaming face!

Their favorite MO (*Modus operandi*—method of operation) is to attack at midday, shape-shifting into the form of a beautiful young woman to waylay travelers at crossroads, or to seduce young men.

Empousa kisses the dude, and he's immediately rendered paralyzed, unable to move! The voracious fiend then feasts while her dinner is still conscious, slurping down all his blood and gnawing on the flesh until nothing is left but cleaned bones! Rank!

Case Study 774/2E

Since kicking off in 1998, speed dating is a somewhat kooky way some adults try to find "the perfect partner."

Groups of men and women get together and take turns talking to one another. The twist is that they only have three to eight minutes, depending on the rules of the event, to decide whether they like someone before moving on to the next "date." We know, crazy!

The popular woman's magazine Scarlett recently ran a piece on one such speed-dating event . . . with a somewhat shocking ending!

The Speed of Love

By Fall N. Forue

The Banquet of Love event was small by usual speed-dating standards. For starters, there were only two women to "date" the twenty young men in attendance.

I'm no bulldog in the looks department, but the other woman attending was an absolute knockout!

I had come here to see if this "aggressive dating" actually works.

This meant having to listen to a constant stream of pimple-faced guys boring me rigid with boasts about how great they were.

With only three minutes a date, at least the time went fast. As the bell rang to change dates, I noticed that the number of men was slowly diminishing.

Those I had chatted with joined the line waiting to speak to the other woman. But the guys who had dated her kept disappearing! Within moments of a man sitting opposite her, she would reach over and kiss him hard on the lips! Then the guy's eyes glazed over, and she led him into a back room . . . returning alone minutes later with her lipstick glistening an even brighter red!

Within the hour, the event had run out of steam——and men! As I was leaving, I asked the woman, who said her name was Emmie (and who, I have to say, had a rank personal hygiene problem!), if she liked speed-dating.

"Oh, yes, dearie!" she cackled, her face, for one brief moment, taking on an almost donkeylike visage. "It's like fast food——delicious!"

That night, the news reported that a huge pile of gnawed adult-male bones had been found in an alley behind the hall that had held the speed-dating event!

It's lucky those men left when they did!

EMPOUSA FACT FILE

Location: Greece
Appearance: Beautiful young woman; donkey/ox/dog features with flaming hair; hideous hag with flaming face and snake hair, one leg of copper and the other that of an ass or of cow dung. Either demoness or ethereal ghost. Or both!
Strength: Lip-smacking powerful!
Weaknesses: This one's a real doozy! Call her a nasty name . . . and she'll run away, crying! (Oh, man! Whadda wimpette!)
Powers: Flight, shape-shifting, paralysis kiss
Fear Factor: 47 (Unless you insult her, in which case: 0!)

HOW TO KILL EMPOUSA

Chase her into a field during a violent storm. Copper being an excellent conductor of electricity, her leg will act like a lightning rod and——ZZZZKK!

From a demon with the head of a mule to a murderous mutilated mule with no head at all!

Hailing from Brazil, the world's fifth-largest country both in size and population (last head count, 198,300,000), the Headless Mule is a sixteenth century woman who broke one of the gazillion religious rules was transformed by an irate god or some such other mystical mage to spend all eternity as a decapitated *Equus mulus*!

Rules, such as? Well, the usual little things like sacrilege (insulting a sacred person or object), dating a priest, infanticide (killing a child), and . . . cannibalism! More specifically, eating her own kid! Hmm, that would do it!

Culinary note: Cannibalism is actually quite common in humans—well, vegetarians and vegans aside, obviously! *Homo antecessor*—the earliest European humans dating back

800,000 to 1.2 million years ago—regularly chomped down on each other. The brains of children especially were considered a yummy delicacy.

Neanderthals—*Homo neanderthalensis*—did likewise, as did early *Homo sapiens*—that's us!

More recently, cannibalism took place during what became known as the Great Famine of China (1959 to 1961), which many think resulted in between thirty and forty five *million* people starving to death; and as recently as 2014, malnourished villagers in North Korea were suspected of killing and eating their own kids to survive! Yum!

Cursed to appear weekly from sundown Thursday to sunrise Friday and to ride through seven parishes, the Headless Mule (aka Mula Sem Cabeça in Portuguese, the official language of Brazil) is scoped as being a ginormous black or brown mule with blazing fire where her head should be!

Others claim she has a mule's head and belches fire from her nostrils!

Her horseshoes are silver, iron, or steel, and make an unearthly racket as she gallops towards her terrified victim!

If some poor sap—human or animal—accidentally walks in front of a Christian cross at a crossroads at midnight, the Headless Mule will materialize.

Letting out a blood-freezing "NEIIIIGH!" (yes, she cries out *without* a head! We're talking spooksville, here! These blockheads make up their own rules!) HM attacks, trampling her intended victim to a bloody pulp before sucking off their fingernails and sucking out their eyeballs! (Sweet!)

You have a couple of cool options to lift the curse.

Option A: Prick her skin with a pin to draw blood, and she will transform back to human. (A major drawback to this is that you then have to live in the same parish as the woman, and the moment you move elsewhere or die, the curse kicks in again!)

Option B: Catch her and tie her to a cross. She'll turn woman once more—but only until sunrise!

Option C: Take off her bridle and she'll remain human until some dope puts it back around her mouth!

Either way, she'll materialize totally naked, sweaty, and smelling of sulfur. If you're a dude, she'll be so grateful, she'll marry you! (Whether you want to or not!)

Case Study 005/8HM

The freaking amazeballs yearly Rio Carnival is also the world's biggest! Dating back to 1723, this energetic, raucous, riotous, and eyeball-blinding colorful fiesta takes place the week before Lent in Rio de Janeiro, Brazil's second largest city.

For six cray-cray, party-filled days and nights, the two million people a day who attend eat, drink, sing, dance, and dress up in glitzy costumes! Mental!

Al Paca, presenter of the award-winning kid's wildlife show It's a Wild Wild World, recently sent co-presenter Carrie Boo a postcard from the Rio Carnival!

Hi, Carrie!

This place is INSANE!! I've had NO sleep in FIVE DAYS!! And knocked back copious amounts of Caipirinha—the Brazilians' favorite alcoholic drink!

I've danced the samba, rode on—and fallen off—a float, played a steel drum—badly!—and been cautioned by the police for running naked through the streets! (I really must cut back on the Caipirinha! Oooh! My head!)

But it hasn't been all play! No, siree, Bob! Somehow I've managed to film Sabiá-laranjeira——Rufous-bellied thrush to you and me!——the country's national bird since 2002. This bird, with its distinctive reddish-orange belly, is renowned for its beautiful song. Our viewers will love it!

But I have even MORE exciting news! Carrie, I've discovered a NEW species never before recorded!!!

It's a mule! With no head! But——it's alive! (No I'm NOT hallucinating! I swear it's true!!)

It appeared during yesterday's parade through the Sambódromo, the area where most people gather to watch the Carnival!

The creature was cantering through the streets, its head-stump ablaze with an eerie light! Thinking some cruel person had set an animal on fire, I rushed over to put out the flames, tripped, and accidentally scratched the mule's flank with my fingers, causing it to bleed!

The animal immediately transformed into a . . . um . . . beautiful, if smelly, naked woman who wrapped her arms around me, pledging her undying love!

Now she wants us to marry or she'll turn back into a headless mule and haunt me forevermore!

I really REALLY wish you were here!!!

Helllllp!!!

Al xxx

HOW TO DEFEAT A HEADLESS MULE

HEADLESS MULE FACT FILE

Location: Brazil
Appearance: Decapitated mule with fiery stump!
Strength: Accursed!
Weaknesses: If you lie facedown on the ground, hiding teeth, nails, and anything else that may shine, being mondo nearsighted—because she, like, has no head!—she'll ignore you!
Powers: Materialization, battle hooves
Fear Factor: 61

"*O*d's blood!" curs'd I, upon viewing the dank depraved Abomination towering before me. "Thy vile canker-blossom'd countenance curdles fresh milk and sours beer!"
Standing somewhat unsteadily within a leaking rowboat on a semi-

The five lands that make up the Nordic countries–Denmark, Finland, Iceland, Norway, and Sweden–have some of the most twisted *freakiweird* ghouls, demons, and rip-out-your-guts-and-squish-your-eyeballs creepoids on a monster hunter's to-kill list!

The *capo di tutti capi* (Italian for "boss of all bosses," better known as Da Godfather!) of Nordic netherworld horrors is the breed of murderous shape-shifting water spirits known by a tsunami of handles but which we've collectively lumped together as—Nøkken!

These flagitious (villainous!) fay can be found anywhere there is water . . . so, basically, *everywhere*! But especially in and around lakes, streams, rivers, ponds, pools, docks, and wells, and they come in a variety of forms and sizes.

If a Nøkk (singular form) is out to kill a young woman, it appears as a handsome, naked young man singing harmoniously while playing a harp, fiddle, or violin. The hypnotic singing brings the woman to the water's edge for the Nøkk to pull under and drown!

If the victim is male, the Nøkk will transform into a beautiful young woman, with similar results!

In Finland, a Nøkk also appears beautiful, but only from the front. Its backside is hairy and grody to the extreme! Or it might disguise itself as an ugly fisherman who turns into a beautiful young woman with three breasts; or perhaps a silvery fish or a large dog.

(Random travel note: The Sami people of Finland use a unit of measurement called a *poronkusema*. This is the distance a reindeer can travel before it needs to pee! For real!)

Other Nordic Nøkken disguises include a wooden boat, log, tree stump, treasure, or a pure white horse. Children are tricked into climbing on the horse's back before it leaps into the river, sending them to a watery grave!

A Nøkk's real form is hideous! (Check out the case study for more intel!)
But don't despair—we've got a cray-cray, crackerjack way to defeat them!

Case Study 427/60N

When hippopotamus-size psycho-evil English tyrant King Henry VIII died in 1547, there was great rejoicing across the land. And who can blame them?

Tens of thousands died under Henry's cruel rule. In 1536 he dissolved all the Catholic monasteries, stealing the land and wealth for himself.

One ticked-off Franciscan friar, William Peyto (d. 1558 or 1559), put a curse on Henry, saying that "God's judgements were ready to fall upon his head and that dogs would lick his blood, as they had done to Ahab!"

During the fortnight (two-week) trip to inter (put in a tomb) Henry's body at St. George's Chapel in Windsor, the funeral procession stopped at Syon Monastery on the River Thames, one of the monasteries that Henry had closed down.

Overnight, a buildup of gases inside Henry's rotting, bloated corpse caused both body and lead casket to burst open, Henry's foul-stinking blood and pus flowing out onto the floor.

The next morning, priests found a stray mangy dog licking up the leaking bodily fluids!

Now that's payback!

One of those deposed friars left England and began a life of religious monster-slaying.

Yes, Brother Jacob fans! We proudly present another entry in our mad monk's thirteen-volume opus, wherein he battles a Nøkk!

THE ADVENTURES OF BROTHER JACOB

"'Od's blood!" curs'd I, upon viewing the dank depraved abomination towering before me. "Thy vile canker-blossom'd countenance curdles fresh milk and sours beer!"

Standing somewhat unsteadily within a leaking rowboat on a semi-frozen lake in Norway, I, by my troth, felt somewhat afeared, for before me was a Satan-birthed creature from the putrefying depths lower than Hell itself!

Its form was most monstrous, with saucer-size, sulfurous glowing eyes, dagger-sharp teeth, and a brine-stinking body of thick matted sea grass!

"I am NØKK!" bellowed the creature most forcefully, raising its mighty fists to smite me. "Thou art a mortal, so thou must DIIIIE!!"

"And I am Father Jacob!" contested I. "If aught shalt perish this morn, suckling of Beelzebub's bosom, it shalt be——THEE!"

With the righteous cry of the warrior priest, I leapt from the boat, swinging wide my trusty battle-ax!

Its blade cleav'd the NØKK in twain before my momentum sent me sinking deep beneath the freezing waters!

My mind growing numb, my eyes closed, and with faint heart, I knew that my Lord's most reverent disciple was to reach the Promised Land anon!

So 'twas with much distress that I awoke in a hut some distance from the lake. Fishermen, spying me thus leaping from the boat, had rescued me!

They believed that the natural gases in the lake made me imagine the Nøkk, for of its remains there wast no sign.

But I knew better, and basked, contented, in the glory of the Lord!

Hallelujah!

NØKKEN FACT FILE

Location: Nordic countries
Appearance: Ask Father Jacob!
Strength: Hideous!
Weaknesses: When a Nøkk attacks, gob a lugie and throw a metal pin or Christian cross into the water while shouting "Nyk! Nyk! Naal i vatn! Jomfru Maria kastet styaal i vatn! Du sæk, æk flyt!" which translates to: "Nøkk! Nøkk! Needle in the water! The Virgin Mary threw steel in the water! You are sinking, I float!" This will kill it stone dead!
Powers: Shape-shifting, invisibility
Fear Factor: 60

HOW TO KILL A NØKK

Wait until it's in fallen-log form and then let loose those superpowered giant termites you've been breeding in your secret laboratory!

You remember how terrifying maniacal monster munchkins can be? (The Philippines-based demonic baby Tiyanak, anyone?!)

Well, here's another cannibalistic brat to add to the list!

Spreading cold-sweat terror throughout the nine thousand–plus citizens that make up the Arapaho nation of Colorado, Nebraska, Oklahoma, and Wyoming in the USA, the misanthropic (human-hating) Raw Gums strikes without mercy, killing and eating his prey until all that is left is bare bones!

(Culture note: The Arapaho nation—Hinono'eino or Inuna-ina, which means "our people" or "people of our kind"—dates back at least three thousand years, when they used to hang out around the Great Lakes and Red River Valley in Manitoba and Minnesota.)

And ol' Raw Gums has one heck of an origin story!

Born in a tipi (aka tepee) to Arapaho parents, baby Raw Gums was a freaki weird kid from the get-go. Aside from his grotesque, swollen bloodred lips, he slept all day and was never seen to eat *anything*! Zip! Nada! Nothing!

But each night, he would sneak out of his cot and crawl his way to one of the other Arapaho camps in the forest. Then, after psychotically strangling the camp's chieftain, Raw Gum would scarf him down as a midnight snack!

The puzzled Arapaho couldn't understand why all their great chieftains had disappeared!

It was five years and a great many missing chieftains later before Raw Gums's parents—who were, like, kind of slow on the uptake—finally figured out why their angelic cherub looked so fit and healthy when he was still refusing any meals!

One morning, while Raw Gums was sleeping off the feast from the night before, they saw fresh blood around his mouth and human flesh sticking out between his teeth! Yep, Raw Gums had forgotten to floss before going to bed! Oops!

Gathering all the camps together, his guilt-tripping pop revealed all! The aghast tribe members swiftly decided—the kid had to go!

Snatching up the wailing little snot, they covered him in animal fat and threw him to a pack of starving dogs!

Bad move, dudes! Before the dogs could attack, Raw Gums used his demonic powers to morph into a young man. Seriously peeved at his unkind and totally undeserved treatment, he called up the skeletal remains of the chieftains he'd killed and ordered them—to attack!

Well, like all brave warriors when faced with over one hundred Undead skeletons clattering toward them, the Arapaho took to the hills!

All, that is, save one! The kooky medicine woman White Old Woman challenged Raw Gums to a duel! And to the loser—death!

Which was unfortunate for White Old Woman because Raw Gums used his powers to cheat. (Hey, he's a demon! What did she think he was gonna do? Play fair?! Sheesh!) He won the challenge and celebrated by cracking open her head with a rock and feasting on her brains!

And he's been doing the same ever since!

Case Study 909/7RG

In our never-ending quest to bring you the latest top secret intel on monster sightings, we regularly hack into communications data banks to sneak a peek at the gazillions of instant messages sent daily worldwide.

What do you mean, that's illegal? If the US government's National Security Agency (NSA) can do it, so can we! Big Brother rules! (Sometimes it's not only monsters we need to be scared of!)

Here is part of a frantic Instant Message (IM) conversation between a young Arapaho dude and his two BFFs about an attack by Raw Gums on his Wyoming reservation!

And for those of you who—like us!—confuse your LOL with your LMAO, here is a "text speak" handy checklist!

SRY 4: Sorry for SRSLY: Seriously UDS: Ugly domestic scene
YT?: You there? ZUP: What's up? WUW: What do you want?
ZZZZ: Sleep GTTU: Got to tell you 2NTE: Tonight
TMTH: Too much to handle TFD: Totally freaked
NFW: No freaking way ^5: High-five H&K2U: Hugs and kisses to you
WGD?: What's going down? WH5: Who, what, where, when, why
WK: Who knows YR: Yeah, right WIB: My word is my bond (the truth)
8: Ate OMGYGTBKM: Oh my God you've got to be kidding me

text NOW
Nakos Little Raven, Mitch Sweeney, Emily Schaffenberger
CONVERSATION
(invited by Nakos Little Raven)

txt **textNOW**

Nakos Little Raven, Mitch Sweeney, Emily Schaffenberger

CONVERSATION
(invited by Nakos Little Raven)

Nakos Little Raven (TRACKER) 2.17AM
SRY 4 late call. SRSLY UDS! YT?

Mitch Sweeney (COOLDUDE) 2.18AM
ZUP, bird? WUW?

Nakos Little Raven (TRACKER) 2.18AM
GTTU 2NTE, TMTH! TFD!

Mitch Sweeney (COOLDUDE) 2.19AM
Split, d00d. ZZZZs calling.

Nakos Little Raven (TRACKER) 2.19AM
Our Res was attacked! By the freakin'

Reply | Send

Nakos Little Raven (TRACKER)   2:17AM
SRY 4 late call. SRSLY UDS! YT?

Mitch Sweeney (COOLDUDE)   2:18AM
ZUP, bird? WUW?

Nakos Little Raven (TRACKER)   2:18AM
GTTU 2NTE, TMTH! TFD!

Mitch Sweeney (COOLDUDE)   2:19AM
Spit, d00d. ZZZZs calling.

Nakos Little Raven (TRACKER)   2:19AM
Our Res was attacked! By the freakin' demon Raw Gums!!!

Mitch Sweeney (COOLDUDE)   2:20AM
NFW!!!

Emily Schaffenberger has joined the conversation
(invited by Nakos Little Raven)

Emily Schaffenberger (HOTSTUFF)   2:21AM
^5 guys! H&K2U. WGD? WH5?

Mitch Sweeney (COOLDUDE)   2:22AM
Bird-demon-res-2NTE-WK!

Emily Schaffenberger (HOTSTUFF)   2:23AM
YR!

Nakos Little Raven (TRACKER)   2:23AM
WIB!! RG killed our chieftain——& 8 him!

Mitch Sweeney (COOLDUDE)   2:25AM
Emily Schaffenberger (HOTSTUFF)   2:25AM
OMGYGTBKM!!!!!!!!!!!!!!!!!!

RAW GUMS FACT FILE

Location: Wherever an Arapaho calls home!
Appearance: Gnarly-looking hellion with oversize blood-colored lips
Strength: He can beat grown men in a wrestling deathmatch, so . . .
Weaknesses: Poisoned lip balm
Powers: Shape-shifting, magic
Fear Factor: 73.3

CAPTURE RAW GUMS AND . . .

When an oily politician visits your area to kiss babies and win votes, introduce him to Raw Gums instead!

THE HISTORY OF—
HERMITAGE CASTLE

Where's the best place to go monster-hunting? Our money's on Britain and Ireland!

These islands off the northwest coast of Europe have more supernatural creatures—both the friendly and the extremely deadly!—per square inch than any other country!

Another twilight terror to add to the Brits' woe list are Red Caps, murderous depraved dwarves (or gruesome goblins, take your pick!) who you'll find chillaxin' in dark and dingy abandoned castles and fortified watchtowers where death-filled bloody battles once took place along the English-Scottish border!

These grade-A, insane freakzoids look like scrawny and shriveled, diminutive old men with leathery skin, glowing red eyes, and long white beards. Their hands are flesh-ripping, oversize eagle's talons, their protruding teeth, dagger-fangs!

Don't be fooled by the heavy iron boots they wear. Moving in a blur of motion, they'll be on you before you can blink, smashing your head in with their diabolical footwear!

But the most noticeable fashion accessory is the red pointy cap perched on each of their heads. Why? Because the hats are made from human skin and dyed with fresh human blood!

A Red Cap (aka Bloody Cap, for obvious reasons!) waits for an unwary traveler to pass by, or culture-junkie tourist to visit the castle ruins, and then—he strikes!

Favorite attack modes include pushing his victims off the ramparts, rolling a boulder down a cliff, slicin' 'n' dicin' them with the razor-sharp scythe or pikestaff he always carries with him, or viciously ripping them to shreds with his deadly teeth and claws!

After drinking his fill of warm, flowing blood, this cackling dacnomanic (obsessed with killing) demon soaks his hat in the icky goo!

And Red Caps' bloodlust is overwhelming! For if their hideous headwear ever dries out, they die! So they need a kill ratio of at least one human a day!

Case Study 557/75R

Here's the text from a pamphlet produced for tourists visiting Hermitage Castle, the most malignant castle in Scotland (seriously, no kidding! Look it up!)—and home to the most terrifying Red Cap of them all!

THE HISTORY OF HERMITAGE CASTLE

The castle was first built in 1240 by Lord Nicolas de Soulis, a cruel tyrant who treated the peasants with appalling bestiality.

But his own barbarous acts were as nothing compared to his descendant Lord William de Soulis. Completely mad, William worshipped Satan, performed witchcraft, and spent his nights carrying out depraved acts and unspeakable tortures on both animals and humans. He was joined in his rabid debauchery by his familiar (a supernatural entity) and only friend, Robin Red Cap.

Lord William was put to death in 1320 by Robert the Bruce, King Robert I of Scotland (1274—1329) for attempted regicide (murder of a monarch), and Robin Red Cap stayed alone in the castle guarding Soulis's hidden treasure. Until, that is, he came face-to-face with the famous Victorian monster hunter, Lady Theodora Bennett.

Here is an extract of her journal describing her encounter with this Devil's goblin.

(Wednesday 6th May 1840)

It was, of a fashion, a somewhat coincidental peculiarity that later upon the very day that the citizens of this Great Britain were officially granted allowance to use the world's first-ever adhesive postage stamp——a small rectangle of black paper with the visage of Her Royal Highness, young Queen Victoria, and selling for one penny——that I faced certain demise at the bloody hands of that homicidal supernatural entity Robin Red Cap!

The keening howl of the chill Scottish eventide breeze, raw upon my bare skin, was as naught to the frigidity of blood coursing through my veins at the sight of the the the deformed creature before me upon the high ramparts of Castle Hermitage.

Diminutive in stature, with sallow, crinkled skin; Satan-red eyes; and long, dirty beard, he was attired in iron boots and a bloodred cap, whose source of origin made one, indeed, quite bilious.

"Trespassing ye be; perish ye will!" His words a sibilant hiss, he approached, taloned hands prepared for flesh-rending mischief.

"My good sir!" said I, tipping my hat in mock politeness. "Such consternation of passion is not good for one's health . . . or one's soul; but, that last, I suspect, for you is gravely wanting!"

The brute did then attack, swiping talons toward my unguarded throat!

I, expecting such, twisted the handle of my cane. A blast of concentrated air erupted from the bottom, rising both cane and me to a small height of safety!

"My turn!" I playfully remarked, pressing the small switch on the side of my brass goggles. A tight beam of luminiferous ether shot forth from within the glass. Robin Redcap ducked down, the shot passing safely over his head.

"Missed!" he cackled, before frowning. I pointed to a space behind him.

Turning, he cried out in horror. His cap, struck by said beam, had dried to the utmost brittleness!

"Curse ye!" cried he in melancholy woe, tottering back, clutching his heart, before toppling over the edge of the ramparts into the stygian darkness below!

RED CAP FACT FILE

Location: Castles and watchtowers on the English-Scottish border
Appearance: Tiny, wizened old dude with red cap, all teeth and claw!
Strength: Unnaturally savage!
Weaknesses: Read a psalm from the Holy Bible and the Red Cap shrieks in pain before running off, leaving one single fang behind!
Powers: Super-speed, super-strength
Fear Factor: 85

EPIFAIL USE OF PSALM-READING

EVEN THOUGH I WALK THROUGH THE VALLEY OF THE SHADOW OF DEATH ... MUMBLE ... MUMBLE ... MUMBLE ......

NYAH-NYAH-NYAH-NYAH! I CAN'T HEAR YOU!

Don't you hate it when your buddies or older siblings take some twisted pleasure in destroying your innocent childhood beliefs?

Like telling you that there is no Easter Bunny, that the Tooth Fairy is fake, and that Santa doesn't exist! (Actually, he DOES, and we've met him! Totally cool dude, unlike his child-murdering evil counterpart, Krampus!)

Well, prepare for another shock!

The Sandman *isn't* a kindhearted old dude who comes into your bedroom in the dark of night to sprinkle sleepy-dust over your eyelids to help give you sweet dreams!

That Sandman *is* a fictional character, created by Danish author Hans Christian Andersen (1805–1875) in his 1841 fairy tale "Ole Lukøje." He wrote the story to calm the night fears of wimpy little munchkins terrified of a visit by the *real* Sandman!

Because this freakzoid is a foul and malevolent fairy who does unmentionable bloody and brutal things to kids! (But, hey, we're going to mention them, anyhow!)

The Sandman has been around since time began, and probably even before that!

He's first recorded in Ancient Sumerian cuneiform writings and drawings and named Krakos (meaning "of sand"), and depicted as rising out of the sand on nights of a full moon!

On such nights, he went on a mad kill spree, stealing away exactly thirteen men, women, and kids!

Hanging them upside down naked by their toes over pools of water all in a row, he would patiently skin them alive!

And if anyone managed to survive such hellish tortures, he would then disembowel them, ripping out their still-steaming intestines!

Fast-forward to the present, and the Sandman has changed his MO slightly.

These days he teleports into the bedrooms of kids who won't go to sleep.

Sprinkling sand into their eyes, he delights in watching them rub so hard that—their eyeballs fall out!

While blood pours from their now-hollow sockets, the Sandman collects the eyes and takes them to feed to his own demonic brats in his castle on the crest of the moon!

Or, for a laugh, once he's collected a bagful of eyes, he'll take them to a cemetery, where he'll push them into the eye sockets of the recently deceased, thereby trapping the kids' souls within the rotting bodies forevermore!

But his favorite party trick is to whisper a hypnotic "tick-tock, tick-tock" to send his victims to dreamland before opening their mouths and pouring sand down their throats until they choke to death!

He then carries them off to his cave to eat them at his leisure!

The good news is that he only chooses blond-haired, blue-eyed kids (5–8% of the world population). The rest of us are laughing! Ha! Suckers!

Case Study 911/66S

In the USA, the consumption of Coca-Cola drinks is a shocking 401 cans per person per year, making it fourth in the world after Mexico (745 cans!), Chile (486), and Panama (416).

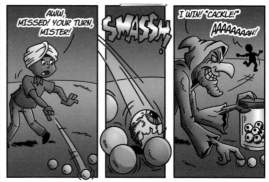

The World Health Organization recommends a total intake of sugar per day of less than one ounce (0.88 ounces) a day. One can of Coke alone has 1.38 ounces! (And the average American consumes 130 pounds of sugar in food and drinks each year!)

And caffeine in fizzy drinks causes anxiety, dizziness, headaches, the jitters, and keeps you from falling asleep. Our advice? Cut down on the sodas!

Here's an extract of a hospital report on a kid who drank too much of a new fizzy drink and paid the penalty with a visit from—The Sandman!

Name of patient: Billy Wendal Timkins   Birthdate: 10-12-2005
Name of Parent/Guardian: Chantelle Timkins (mother)
Address of Parent/Guardian: 204 Trailer Park Lane, Oakland, CA
Physical Examination Results:

The patient was admitted with horrific injuries to his eyes. They appear to have been gouged out, the empty sockets bleeding profusely. The child was screaming uncontrollably and required heavy sedation.

According to police officials called to the crime scene, they found Billy sitting up in his bed at 11:22 p.m., shrieking unintelligibly. He was pleading to something he called the "Sandman" not to kill him, that he would be a good boy and go to sleep when he should. Billy claimed that it was he, Billy, who tore out his own eyes.

Police confirm that the room was strewn with empty cans of a new soda drink called "Zap," the top-selling drink for adolescents. There was no sign of his missing eyes, and police believe they were stolen by the perpetrator of the attack.

Billy is permanently blinded, and will probably need a lifetime of intense psychological therapy in a secure mental institution.

Examining physician: Dr. Payne   Date of examination: March 20, 2015

SANDMAN FACT FILE

Location: North America, Central and Eastern Europe

Appearance: Lanky cloaked dude with decaying, discolored skin, long fingers, claws, and sharp teeth. Or made completely of sand with black eye sockets.

Strength: Totally nightmarish, obviously!

Weaknesses: Wrap a thick scarf around your eyes, nose, and mouth before going to bed. Major drawback? You'll probably suffocate in your sleep!

Powers: Shape-shifting, flight, teleportation, hypnotism. Can enter your dreams to kill you!

Fear Factor: Blond-haired, blue-eyed kids? 99.9

HOW TO ESCAPE THE SANDMAN . . .

. . . if you're blond and blue-eyed!
Hair dye and colored contact lenses!

Anyone who tells you that the spectral, child-murdering creep Slender Man is fake is talking out of their butts!

The dude is REAL, and has been on his nonstop kill spree since at least the early Neolithic Era! (which began around 10,200 BC and ended between 4500 and 2000 BC!)

Take a trip to Serr da Capivara National Park in Brazil and see for yourself!

On a cave wall dating back to at least 9000 BC is parietal art (cave paintings) depicting a creepy elongated human leading away a child by the hand!

If you want more proof, pop along to Egypt and visit the tomb of Pharaoh Wazner (aka Wazenez or Wadjenedj), who ruled the Nile Delta around 3100 BC.

Hieroglyphic carvings show that this royal dude actually fought Slender Man, known back then as the "Thief of the Gods" or the "Thief of Kuk," who was depicted with multiple arms!

And if *that* doesn't convince you (anyone ever tell you that you're very hard to please?!), catch a flight to Germany and check out the extremely detailed (and totally rad!) woodcuts by sixteenth century Renaissance artist Hans Freckenberg (d. 1543). These show a stretched skeletal figure again with multiple upper limbs!

Der Großmann

Slender Man is merely a modern tag for the deformed horror.

The Ancient Babylonians called him Alû. In Germany he's known as Der Großmann (the Tall Man), in Holland Takkenmann (Branch Man). Russia has the Corrector, Japan has Noppera-bō (aka Zumbera-bō), and the Chinese, Hùndùn!

The English are haunted by Clutchbone, while Scottish kids have nightmares about meeting Fear Dubh (the Dark Man)!

In Wales, desperate parents even created a pants-wetting nursery rhyme to warn their kids of the danger of the Faceless One!

'Hush, thy childe, do not stray far from the path
or The Faceless One shall steal you away to Fairieland.
He preys on sinful and defiant souls
and lurks within the woods.
He has hands of ebony branches
and a touch as soft as silk.
Fear The Faceless One, thy childe,
for he shall take you to a dark place.
And what shall become of thou?

Both dolichocercic (having extremely long arms) and dolichocnemic (having extremely long legs), he stands between six and fifteen feet tall, apparently able to stretch his body at will, and occasionally dresses smartly in a black suit, red tie, and fedora!

His features are completely blank, although some reports claim he can morph his face into whatever he wants! He may have two human arms or many, sometimes they are tree branches, and other times, black tentacles!

The Tall Man silently stalks children, waiting for the opportunity to snatch them away and take them to "the dark place"!

There he gleefully and very slowly tortures them before removing their organs while they are still conscious, enjoying their agonizing death screams!

He is always there with you. Hiding in the shadows and in the darkness of night. He never leaves your side, patiently biding his time, waiting for that moment to soundlessly—STRIKE!

Be afraid! Be *very* afraid!

Case Study 323/6TM

Lacking the mindless pleasures of television and social media networks, the mid-sixteenth century saw circus freak shows and exhibitions as the number-one crowd-pullers.

Deformed humans and animals were put on display for the somewhat twisted entertainment of the masses—what we now call reality TV shows!

Freak shows reached their peak in the mid-nineteenth century, when extroverted author, publisher, politician, philanthropist, and showman P.T. Barnum (Phineas Taylor Barnum—1810–1891) established his Grand Traveling Museum, Menagerie, Caravan & Hippodrome, which he proclaimed to be "the Greatest Show on Earth!"

Here's a transcript from an early phonograph recording featuring a ringmaster of a freak show introducing his acts, including one very special—and deadly!—performer!

(Hsss, crackle)

Layyyy-deees and Gentlemen! Boys and Girls! Welcome . . . to the Greatest Freak Show in the Universe!

For your Edacious, Enthusiastic Entertainment and Edification we bring you tonight the most Extravagant Extravagancies and Extraordinary, Eclectic Ephemeromorphs to Embrangle and Edify you that have Ever Existed on Earth!

We have the Illustrious Legendary Legerdemain, the Great Merlin——the Completely Amputated Magician!

The Fabulous Fiji Mermaid with the head and torso of a monkey and the scales and tail . . . of a fish!

The Gruesome and Disgusting . . . Boy with Three Heads!

And last . . . but certainly not least! . . . the Star of our Show! That Eclectic Extravaganza of Efflorescent Ectomorphic Ectoplasm! That Devil Incarnate! The Phthartic, Plangorous Premundane Phantom of Pernoctation!

Ladies, Gentlemen, and Children of All Ages, we proudly present to you the Lygophiliac Lemur of Lucifer himself! The One . . . the Only . . . the Tall Man!

That's right, Tall Man! Stretch those arms and legs! Doesn't he look gross? And those tentacles sprouting from his back are just so cool! Don't panic, folks! Just because he's hypnotizing your kids and drawing them toward him doesn't mean he'll . . . um . . . hurt them . . . ? Er . . . Tall Man . . . what are you doing?! Ab-Absorbing . . . m-melting! . . . the kids . . . inside you . . . ?! Ewww! Revolting! No, don't rip off their heads! Stop! Stop! Nooo! Ahhhhh!!

(Hsss, crackle)

Phonograph Recording Ends

TALL MAN FACT FILE

Location: The world
Appearance: Unnaturally tall, slender, pale dude with no face!
Strength: Mystically inhuman!
Weaknesses: Um . . .
Powers: Elasticity, teleportation, hypnotism, shape-shifting, psychokinesis (can move objects with the power of his mind!), induces madness in his victims, death touch!
Fear Factor: 99.9

HOW TO DEFEAT THE TALL MAN

Grab hold of his long arms and legs and tie him in knots!

We now come to some of the most far-out freakzoids ever covered in our monster series!

How so? Because these dementedly deranged Japanese psycho spirits spend their first one hundred years as ordinary inanimate household objects before springing to murderous Unlife!

These aren't objects that have been enchanted by some mad wizard to attack his enemies. On their one hundredth birthday, they literally become *alive* and self-aware, meaning they can think for themselves! Mental-weird!

Rookie monster hunters should definitely consider capturing some of these cockamamie pint-size poltergeists before aiming for the big guns.

To drop a truth bomb, if you fail against a berserker vegetable grater, what's the chance of bringing down the ninety-foot Chinese skeletal horror Gashadokuro or a maniac Mongolian Death Worm?!

The collective name for these yōkai (ghosts and demons) is indeed Tsukumogami (付喪神—"kami" [spirit] of tool).

Many are annoying pranksters more than bloodthirsty butchers, but even the most placid will be quick to anger if thoughtless humans disrespect them.

Anyone who throws out a Tsukumogami in the garbage is soon going to wish he or she hadn't! Its friends will join forces and take revenge on such wasteful people!

(FYI: The amount of trash thrown out by humans daily and that ends up in landfills instead of being recycled is frankly horrific. All countries are just as bad as their neighbors, although China and America are by far the worst offenders. China creates *one-third* of the world's garbage output! And Americans throw out approximately 260 million TONS of garbage every single year, enough to cover the entire state of Texas twice over! So c'mon, fellow monster hunters! Don't throw away—RECYCLE! Your planet will love you for it!)

A Tsukumogami with a mad-on is terrifying to behold! Ittan-momen, a long strip of white cotton cloth, will glide on the night winds until it locates its prey! Attacking, it wraps itself around the victim's face or neck to suffocate or strangle him!

Likewise, the Shirōnen, which can be either mosquito netting or a dust cloth, flies around a victim's legs to trip him up or enters his mouth while he sleeps, and chokes him to death!

Case Study 997/85T

Our popular Fact File section at the end of each chapter is a quick checklist for monster hunters before going into bloody battle against hideous creatures from humanity's worse nightmares!

We were inspired by similar checklists on the dozens of awesome trading-card games that are available, both as actual cards and on apps. On one side of the card are facts about the subject, be it dinosaurs, machines, planets, monsters, or whatever, and on the back, a short description.

Some people trade cards to complete a set, others play a totally wicked game where players use their cards to beat the data on an opponent's cards.

A Japanese company has recently released its own trading-card pack based on the demonic Tsukumogami! Here are a few of our favorites!

CHŌCHIN-OBAKE

Location: Japan
Strength: Papery
Fear Factor: 3
The Chōchin-obake (提灯お化け)—"paper lantern ghost"—first made an appearance during the Edo period (1603–1867). Living paper lanterns born from demonic anger at being discarded by their owners, they attack travelers at night. The more people they murder, the more souls they collect and the brighter the flame within them grows!

BOROBOROTON

Location: Japan
Strength: Tough
Fear Factor: 71
The Boroboroton (暮露暮露団)—"tattered futon"—is a Japanese sleeping mat with killer moves! Furious at its mistreatment by its owner, who has allowed it to wear out from overuse, it waits for night, and then—attacks! Tossing its sleeping

victim onto the floor, it wraps around his head to either snap his neck or strangle him!

MENREIKI

Location: Japan
Strength: Haunting
Fear Factor: 19
Originating during the reign of Japanese regent Prince Shōtoku (572–622), the Menreiki (面霊気)—"masked essence"—are actors' abandoned masks from the Noh Theater (musical plays that often last all day). Possessed of human souls, these masks haunt theaters, calling out to be loved. Much like European Imps, they are more of a pest than dangerous.

KASA-OBAKE

Location: Japan
Strength: Deadly
Fear Factor: 69
Better known as "the umbrella demons," the Kasa-Obake (傘おばけ) have been whacking people over the head since at least the tenth century. Hopping about on one foot, these Tsukumogami are easily enraged and will attack without mercy. Favorite methods of killing humans are to trap them inside the parasols to suffocate, and beating them to death!

TSUKUMOGAMI FACT FILE

Location: Japan
Appearance: Any household object!
Strength: From wimp to deadly!
Weaknesses: Perform a Japanese Jinja ceremony, such as Hari Kuyou, to make peace with an unwanted or broken Tsukumogami. Otherwise, zap 'em with electricity—it kills 'em stone dead!
Powers: Different for each Tsukumogami!
Fear Factor: Between 3 (Chochin-obake—paper lantern) and 93 (Koinryō—an extremely sharp-clawed staff!)

HOW TO CAPTURE/KILL A TSUKUMOGAMI

There are thousands of them! Take your pick!

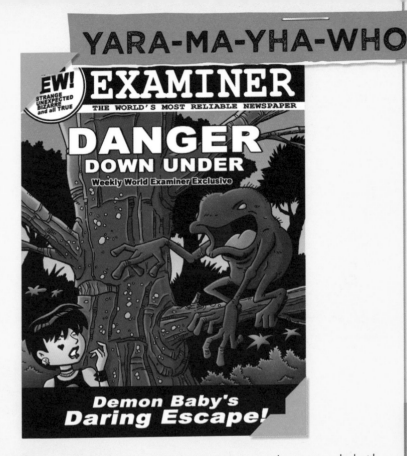

EW! STRANGE UNEXPECTED BIZARRE and all TRUE

EXAMINER
THE WORLD'S MOST RELIABLE NEWSPAPER

DANGER DOWN UNDER
Weekly World Examiner Exclusive

Demon Baby's Daring Escape!

The United Kingdom may have, by numbers, the *most* supernatural creepies to deal with, but the *kookiest* are definitely found nowhere else but in Australia!

And by far, the grossest, most puke-inducing terror Down Under is the dread demonic vampire beast Yara-Ma-Yha-Who, "he who eats his victims"—and then regurgitates them!

Living in Oz (the affectionate name for the country) means facing certain death on an hourly basis! The Aussies and native Aborigines have the deadliest just about *everything*!

The world's most toxic snake (the taipan—one bite and you're pushing up daisies!), jellyfish (the twenty-four-eyed box jellyfish, whose ten-foot tentacles hold some of the world's fastest-acting death venom!), arachnid (the redback spider—only 0.4 inch in size, so easily missed hiding in your shoe . . . until it strikes!), octopus (the five-to-eight-inch-long blue-ringed octopus's bite can kill within minutes!), croc (the saltwater crocodile reaches up to twenty-two feet in length!), and, um . . . a snail!

We kid you not! Cone snails grow to nine inches in length, and their miniscule hollow and barbed teeth inject lethal venom into the skin! In recent years, at least twenty people have died from a snail bite!

To add to their troubles, Aussie kids also have YMYW to contend with!

It's bad enough walking under a fig tree only to be dropped on by a mugly four-foot-high, bloodred megacephalic (enormous-headed), abdominous (large-bellied) creature with a ginormous toothless mouth, leaping from the branches in savage attack-mode!

But then to be drained of blood before being eaten is a bit much!

Before you ask, not *all* vampires drink blood through the mouth! With YMYW, he has toothed suckers on his long tentacled fingers and toes, which he uses for climbing, keeping hold of victims, and, much like a leech, piercing the skin to blood-feast!

But your mental tortures don't end there—no, siree, Bob!—because YMYW, being somewhat of a weight-watcher, goes for an energetic power walk to sweat off his dinner, knowing that you're too weak from blood loss to escape!

When he returns, he lifts up your feet and pushes you, inch by screaming inch, into his cavernous mouth, until there is nothing left!

And then he drinks a glass of water and vomits you right back out again!

But the horror doesn't end, even then! For, your body now shorter and your skin color of a redder hue, he swallows you and pukes you up, repeatedly!

Each time he does so, you shrink, smaller and smaller, your skin turning a darker red, until . . . YOU, too, are now transformed into a Yara-Ma-Yha-Who!! *Aaaaah!*

Case Study 205/96Y

Here's another shocking report from Neela

Nightshade, ace reporter for the Weekly World

Examiner!

PRESS

WEEKLY WORLD EXAMINER

FIELD REPORTER

NEELA NIGHTSHADE

247365 875 236085

OFFICIAL

ACCESS

Danger down under

Weekly World Examiner Exclusive
New South Wales, Australia, April 14

I've come to the small city of Wagga Wagga to investigate sightings of a child-eating demon, and find that I'm being upstaged . . . by a Goth teenager!

"G'day, cobber!" she says, crouching behind a eucalyptus bush, beneath the long branches of a fig tree. "Name's Soul-Gon McDonald. Monster hunter extraordinaire!"

I'm about to return introductions, when she grins broadly. "Holy Dooley! I'm no dill! You're that bottler pommy journo! Spiffy to meet ya!"

"Likewise," I reply, puzzled. "I think!"

"Just waiting for that dunny-rat cookie Yara-Ma-Yha-Who to do the Harold Holt from this tree to hunt up another ankle-biter for his tucker!" Soul-Gon whispers, holding up a roll of what looks like wallpaper. "And then, that bitser's mine!"

The girl is suddenly and painfully body-slammed to the ground by a stout, bright-red horror with huge head and twitching tentacled digits hurtling down from above! The Yara-Ma-Yha-Who!

The prey this demon's hunting—is us!

GRRAAKK! it roars, long tentacled fingers flicking toward Soul-Gon to feed!

"I've got Buckley's chance of surviving this!" she gasps, spinning away to snatch up the roll of paper she has with her. "Unless . . . !"

Unfurling, the paper reveals the other side covered in wet paste!

The demon attacks, its deadly suckers striking the paper—and sticking fast!

GRRAAKK! it screams in frustration, sucking with all its might to break a hole in the paper!

Instead, its body swells up from the effort to gargantuan size and——BANG!

Exploding, the creature's body parts drench Soul-Gon and me in bloody, slimy goo!

"Bonza!" cheers Soul-Gon.

We high-five, grinning.

And I realize that I've found a new ally in my fight against the monsters! Fair dinkum!

And for those of us confused by Aussie slang, here's the translation:

G'day, cobber: Hello, friend; Holy Dooley: Good grief; dill: idiot; bottler: outstanding person; journo: journalist; pommy: English person; spiffy: great; dunny rat: extremely cunning; cookie: cockroach; do the Harold Holt: to bolt, to flee; ankle-biter: little child; tucker: meal; bitser: mongrel; Buckler's chance: no chance; Bonza/Fair dinkum: excellent

YARA-MA-YHA-WHO FACT FILE

Location: Fig and leafy trees (sometimes caves) of Australia

Appearance: Short, heavy red dude with smooth hairless skin, tentacled fingers and toes, and big mouth!

Strength: Prodigious!

Weaknesses: If YMYW doesn't upchuck his meal, the vengeful spirit of the fig tree will kill him!

Powers: World puking champ! Mephitic (totally noxious, foul-smelling), killer gas farts!

Fear Factor: 94.7

HOW TO KILL YARA-MA-YHA-WHO

After he's eaten a kid, superglue his mouth shut. When he strains without success to vomit up his meal, he'll BURST!

GRUESOME CREATURES FACT FILES

ALP-LUACHRA

Location: Ireland

Appearance: Well, when it's not *invisible*, it is a tiny green Unseelie fairy.

Strength: Magical!

Weaknesses: Extremely greedy, careless, and stupid. If you eat *lots* of salted food, Alp-Luachra will fly out of your stomach to quench its desperate thirst.

Powers: Shape-shifting, flight, invisibility, leeching. A parasite (an organism that lives in or on another creature and feeds off them) that shrinks to the size of a small newt or lizard and slips into the open mouth of a human sleeping by a stream. Making its way down into the stomach, the Alp-Luachra sets up its home—even inviting fairy friends to join it in a house-warming party!—consuming all the food that host-person eats until the poor dope wastes away from starvation, and slowly, agonizingly—dies! Dank!

Fear Factor: 76

BINBŌGAMI

Location: Japan

Appearance: A Binbōgami (literally, "kami of poverty"; *kami* means "spirit") is an emaciated (abnormally thin), dirty old dude holding an *uchiwa* (hand-held, folding paper fan).

Strength: Physical strength—none! (It's a spirit!)

Weaknesses: If you light an *iori* (fireplace) on Omisoka (New Year's Eve), it will chase away a Binbōgami and invite in a Fuku-no-kami (the *kami* of good luck).

A plate of freshly cooked miso shaped like a scallop will entice him out, and while he's sniffing the food, slam the plate shut, trapping Binbōgami inside. Then toss the plate into a river to wash him away! Alternatively, pray at a small shrine to welcome Binbōgami into your home, and he will leave twenty-one days later.

Powers: Immortality. (Being a *kami*, he cannot be killed.) Inhabits either a person or his house to bring him abject poverty and misery until the day he dies.

Fear Factor: 63.4

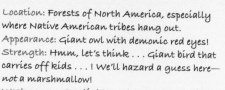

Location: Forests of North America, especially where Native American tribes hang out.

Appearance: Giant owl with demonic red eyes!

Strength: Hmm, let's think . . . Giant bird that carries off kids . . . ! We'll hazard a guess here—not a marshmallow!

Weaknesses: Sunlight—only attacks at night!

Powers: Its name translates to "owner-of-a-bag" for its habit of stuffing screaming and terrified kids into a large sack and flying off with them! You don't want to know what comes next (not if you want to sleep tonight)!

Fear Factor: For the above-mentioned Native Americans—most notably their little munchkins—54.1

BOGEY

Location: Scotland and Ireland

Appearance: Large cat as big as an adult Great Dane dog with white spot on its breast.

Strength: Fairy-cat tough!

Weaknesses: Some cryptozoologists (someone who studies mythological animals) believe the Cait Sith is a witch who can safely change into a cat eight times, but with the ninth transformation she remains a cat—forever! Catnip, ball of wool, music, riddles, tickling behind her ear, or rubbing her tummy will keep her occupied. You must absolutely not have a fire going near a corpse, as the warmth attracts the Cait Sith!

Powers: Soul-stealing—by walking over a corpse before burial! Will turn your cows' milk dry if you don't leave out a saucer of milk for her! (Those of you who own cows, that is!)

Fear Factor: For dead people and farmers—12.3

CAIT SITH

GA-GORIB

Location: Savannas and deserts of southwest Africa, where the native Khoikhoi people (literally "people people" or "real people") hang out. The Khoikhoi—aka Khoi, for short—are closely related to the San (Bushmen) people, both of whom first appeared in South Africa around 25,000 BC. (Nope, we can't be more accurate—we weren't actually around back then to take notes!)

Appearance: Mugly, huge, leopard-spotted troll

Strength: Huge troll-y sort

Weaknesses: Kind of dim. Whack him behind the ear with a sharp stone to kill him. (But make sure your aim is good, because Ga-Gorib will return fire, and he's a perfect shot!)

Powers: Sits on the edge of his massive pit and mouths off insults to passersby, challenging them to throw stones at him. If someone is dumb enough to take up the challenge, this twisted troll will throw a stone back, twice as hard, instantly killing his opponent, who then falls into the pit to be feasted on by Ga-Gorib!

Fear Factor: 52.3

HARPIES

Location: Cemeteries and foul-smelling places full of garbage in Greece

Appearance: Messengers of Hades, the dude who rules—and also the name of—the Underworld! Hungry, filthy, mondo-mugly old women with human chests, feathered bird bodies (sometimes with human arms), bear ears, bronze wings, and sharp, crooked claws. Nice long-flowing hair, though!

Strength: Violent, vicious, mondo-cruel. Can carry off adult humans without working up a sweat!

Weaknesses: A sharp arrow through the head will sort them out!

Powers: Super-speed, flight, strength, voracious appetites, gag-inducing obnoxious smells. (Their BO is to die for—literally!) Creating powerful winds, sea storms, and totally bad weather. Deafening screeching, soul-stealing, food-robbing—they'll poop a foul one on your plate to put you off eating your dinner! (That would do the trick!) Swoop down to take people who don't want to die to the Underworld (basically everyone, then!); steal away kids and adults to torture and torment by scratching out their eyes and ripping off their flesh! Nauseous!

Fear Factor: 82.8

MOKOI

Location: Arnhem Land, Australia. (Arnhem Land is one of five regions in the Northern Territory. Approx. 310 miles from Darwin, capital city of Australia. Inhabited by the Yolngu people, some of Australia's original inhabitants. Population: approx. 16,200. The world's oldest-known stone ax, at least 35,000 years old, was found here! Bodacious!)

Appearance: Small, evil, shape-shifting spirits. (So your guess is as good as ours!)

Strength: Physically, a powder puff—but all magical!

Weaknesses: Counter-magic!

Powers: Magic. (Note: They kill human sorcerers who use dark magic!) Disease-spreadings, bad luck-zapping (causing fatal accidents!), hypnosis. (And they lead kids away at night to eat them!)

Fear Factor: 57

PSOGLAV

Location: A "dark land with plenty of gemstones, but no sun"! Also in caves of Serbia, Montenegro, and Croatia, in southern Europe. Yugoslavia was originally made up of six nations: Slovenia, Croatia, Macedonia, Bosnia & Herzegovina, Serbia, and Montenegro—and lasted from 1918 until 1992. Capital city (Serbia): Belgrade. Capital city (Montenegro): Podgorica. Capital city (Croatia): Zagreb. Population (Serbia): 7,181,505. Population (Montenegro): 622,777. Population (Croatia): 4,284,889.

Appearance: You want bizarre? We'll give ya BIZARRE! How about . . . a dog's head with iron teeth—yep, iron teeth!!—and one eye in the middle of the forehead, a human body, long talons, and a horse's legs!

Strength: Large dog. (Hey, you ever been savaged by a Saint Bernard?! Those mutts are lethal!)

Weaknesses: Rubber bones—they can chew them for hours!

Powers: Eating people, alive or dead! The dead ones they dig up from graves to chow down on, no matter how old and rank they may be! (We'll pass, thanks!)

Fear Factor: 66.4

RAKSHASA

Location: India and the Federal Democratic Republic of Nepal. (Nepal is a sovereign state in South Asia, located in the Himalayas mountain range.)

Appearance: Enormous demon dudes with flaming red eyes and hair, two protruding mouth fangs, and razor-sharp fingernails. They change their appearance to suit their moods. One day a monster, the next an animal. Females turn into beautiful women known as Manushya-Rakshasi. Their king, Rāvana, is the most powerful—and sports ten heads! (Must take all day to wash his hair! Sheesh!)

Strength: Super-powerful during the evening, especially during the dark period of the new moon.

Weaknesses: The rising sun (they only appear at night!), prayers, and sacrifices! (We suggest trying the prayer route first! All that blood—ick!)

Powers: Shape-shifting, invisibility, flight, illusion spells. Ferocious man-eaters—they are so voracious, they even tried chowing down on Brahma, the Hindu deva (god) of creation! Hardcore!

Fear Factor: 93.9

SHADHAVER

Location: Forests and deserts of the Islamic Republic of Iran in the Middle East. (Iran borders the Gulf of Oman, the Persian Gulf, and the Caspian Sea, between Iraq and Pakistan. Before 1935, Iran was called Persia, one of the oldest and most influential civilizations, ruling over most of the known world and dating back to at least 550 BC! Size of Iran: 638,393 square miles. Capital city: Tehran. Population: 76,424,450. Language: Persian.)

Appearance: Beautiful golden unicorns with black markings around the eyes. (Makes a change from the buglies we're always tracking down!)

Strength: Total cuteness! Ahh!

Weaknesses: Can't resist collecting the latest My Little Pony merchandise! (And who can blame them?! We love those colorful ponies, too!)

Powers: When the wind blows, it enters the unicorn's horn, creating an alluring, hypnotic melody that enchants all who hear it—animals and humans. As its prey draws near, Shadhavar's features turn demonical, and—cackling evilly!—it attacks, kicking or stabbing to death its victims before eating them!

Fear Factor: 33.3

TEKE-TEKE

Location: Japan

Appearance: Bloody upper torso of a schoolgirl or young woman pulling herself along on arms and elbows, carrying a scythe or large saw. This onryō (怨霊)—vengeful spirit—died a particularly gruesome death when she fell onto a train track and was sliced in half by a speeding train! She's now back to terrorize the living! (Go, girl!)

As she pulls herself along using her clawlike fingers, her body makes a rather disturbing teke-teke sound! Her name is Kashima Reiko, supposedly some strange Japanese "abbreviation" of Kamen Shinin Ma, meaning "mask" or "dead-person demon."

Strength: Half of what it was when she was alive, we'd imagine!

Weaknesses: When she asks, "Where are my legs?" answer, "At the Meishin Railway," and when she then asks, "Who told you this?" reply, "Kashima Reiko!" She will then let you live. If ya don't . . . (See below)

Powers: Moving at a frightening pace, attacking unsuspecting kids at dusk. If they get her questions wrong, she slices them in half with her scythe, turning them into yet another Teke-Teke!

Fear Factor: Kids coming home from school: 97.5

TLAHUELPUCHI

Location: Mexico, and El Salvador in South America, specifically the indigenous (original inhabitants of a country) Nahua peoples. (The Nahuas are better known as the Aztecs).

Appearance: Bloodthirsty Undead vampire witch or human (usually female—there are a few males, but they're kind of wimps!) who can shape-shift into a glowing animal, preferably a turkey or a vulture, but also a flea, cat, or dog. These most evil ones detach their legs before hunting, for swifter movement.

Strength: Hypnotic stare!

Weaknesses: Must feed at least once a month, or die. Metal, garlic, and onions keep them at bay!

Powers: Flight, shape-shifting, magic, hypnosis. They choose a human victim who's at home, and then perform a ritual, flying over the house in the shape of a cross. This done, they are able to pass through the walls as a mist to begin the bloody feast!

Fear Factor: 91.6